Any Day with you

ALSO BY MAE RESPICIO

The House That Lou Built

Any Day with you

MAE RESPICIO

WENDY
LAMB
BOOKS

Text copyright © 2020 by Mae Respicio
Jacket art copyright © 2020 by Rebecca Mock
Interior art copyright © 2020 by Mark Koerner

All rights reserved. Published in the United States by Wendy Lamb Books, an imprint of Random House Children's Books, a division of Penguin Random House LLC, New York.

Wendy Lamb Books and the colophon are trademarks of Penguin Random House LLC.

Visit us on the Web! rhcbooks.com

Educators and librarians, for a variety of teaching tools, visit us at RHTeachersLibrarians.com

Library of Congress Cataloging-in-Publication Data
Names: Respicio, Mae, author.
Title: Any day with you / Mae Respicio.
Description: First edition. | New York : Wendy Lamb Books, [2020] |
Summary: During the summer before seventh grade, Kaia, who enjoys living in Southern California, visiting the beach with her family, and creating movie make-up effects, makes a film with her friends to win a contest and hopefully prevent her beloved great-grandfather from moving back to the Philippines.
Identifiers: LCCN 2019023201 (print) | LCCN 2019023202 (ebook) |
ISBN 978-0-525-70757-8 (hardcover) | ISBN 978-0-525-70758-5 (library binding) |
ISBN 978-0-525-70760-8 (paperback) | ISBN 978-0-525-70759-2 (ebook)
Subjects: CYAC: Family life—California—Los Angeles—Fiction. | Filipino Americans—Fiction. | Great-grandfathers—Fiction. | Motion pictures—Production and direction—Fiction. | Los Angeles (Calif.)—Fiction.
Classification: LCC PZ7.1.R465 An 2020 (print) | LCC PZ7.1.R465 (ebook) | DDC [Fic]—dc23

The text of this book is set in 11- point Aleo.
Interior design by Heather Kelly

Printed in the United States of America
10 9 8 7 6 5 4 3 2 1
First Edition

FOR MY SWEET BOYS,
ALDEN AND CAEL

1

I know the ocean first by smell, then by sight. It's how my family always does it.

Sunlight floods our car as we wind up the Pacific Coast Highway. Once we near the beach Dad rolls down the windows and says, "Everyone breathe it all in!"

My big sister, Lainey, snorts loudly the way she does whenever Dad says that, and we crack up.

I close my eyes and inhale softly; it smells like morning and seaweed. That's when I spot it: miles and miles of glittering water.

We pull into a small parking lot. Mom, Dad, and Lainey unload our gear while I help my little brother, Toby, out of his car seat. Then a short walk down a rickety wooden staircase. As soon as we touch bottom I kick off my flip-flops and we pad along, the sand soft and warm under my feet. We plonk down our things.

"Ah, perfect," Mom says, shaking out a blanket that floats in midair.

Toby grabs his shovel and starts digging. Lainey and Dad yank surfboards out of their long cozies. And I do what I always do: trace a heart and plant myself in the center of it.

Around us the beach is already packed with colorful umbrellas, kids building castles, and surfers bobbing in the distance. Waves lap in gently.

Among all these people I'm a dot and nothing more. I imagine a movie camera looking down on me, then zooming out-out-out as wide and far as it can go until it reaches a million miles away and I dissolve into a small blue marble. The Earth.

I'm not sure why it's called Earth instead of Ocean, since most of our planet is covered by water. I learned that from Tatang, my ninety-year-old great-grandfather—he feeds facts to me like candy. Tatang taught middle school and knows everything.

In his younger days, Tatang used to swim and free-dive in the Philippines, where he grew up. He'd come across animals like the psychedelic frogfish or the blue-ringed octopus, so wondrous they seem more like mythical creatures from the Filipino folktales he loves to tell. I've looked them up to try to sketch them, but I'm sure it's not the same as seeing them up close.

Lainey sits next to me and I rest my head on her shoulder.

Dad sighs. "Our last family beach day before Dr. Lainey leaves, huh, girls?"

"I can't wait," Lainey says.

"Hey!" Dad says.

"I mean…yeah, I'm really going to miss you guys," she says with a big grin.

Next week Lainey's crossing the ocean—all the way to the Philippines—to study abroad for the summer. Then in the fall she's off to college in New York. Premed.

"You're going to have an amazing time, sweetheart," Mom says.

At the end of Lainey's high school valedictorian speech, the crowd gave her a standing ovation, and my family cheered the loudest. Tatang even brought a megaphone and shouted, "Way to go, Elena!"

Impressing people is my sister's talent. Sometimes I get a little jealous. I've never done anything that people gush over.

Lainey nudges my side. "How you doing, Kaia? You're kind of quiet."

"You'll miss the solar eclipse," I say. It's at the end of the summer and she won't be back in time.

"The Philippines should have an eclipse, too, right? I thought we all shared the same moon and sun?" She gives me a teasing smile.

"No, I mean here. Tatang is taking us to the science museum. They pass out special glasses so we won't hurt our eyes."

"That sounds like fun," Mom says. "I'm sure he's dying to tell us a new bakunawa story."

"The sea serpent who causes eclipses! I love that one," I say.

Everything I know about Filipino creatures comes from Tatang and Mom, since Tatang's basically a walking encyclopedia and Mom teaches Asian American studies at a big university. They could tell stories nonstop. Tatang's favorite is about the bakunawa, a giant sea serpent with a mouth as wide as a lake, who swallows suns and moons—until villagers scare him back into the water by banging on pots, pans, and drums.

Whenever we see a partial moon, he likes to say, "Bakunawa's been hungry."

I'm old enough now to know that magical monsters don't cause eclipses. A total solar eclipse is rare; it happens when the moon completely covers the sun. What's cool is this will be my very first one.

I picture the sun going down here in Los Angeles and all of the beach-loving Angelenos freaking out and fleeing every which way like the world's ending. We'll only be able to see a partial eclipse, but it'll be fun to watch it with Tatang. Some kids at school think I'm weird for hanging out with a senior citizen, but I don't mind. Once people get to know my great-grandpa they understand why he's my best adventure buddy.

Lainey kneels by her surfboard and rubs it with a small bar of wax. "What do you think would happen if the sun disappeared entirely?" she asks.

"Ooh, I know this one," I say. "We wouldn't immediately

turn cold and shrivel up and die, but things would *definitely* be *different*."

Mom smiles at me. "How so?"

"Well, there'd be no photosynthesis for the plants, so we'd run out of oxygen, and then the oceans would freeze and the bottom levels of the food chain would die off and we'd all turn into scavengers living off the dead, sunless bodies of other beings for mere survival!"

Dad, Lainey, and I burst out laughing.

"Aww, I wish I could watch the eclipse with you, Kai-Kai, but remember what Tatang always says." Lainey clears her throat, stretches her arms like she's hugging the air, and in her best imitation of our great-grandfather's deep voice says: "Kaia, we all share the same sky, so when you're looking up, you will know that I am too." She shakes her finger at me. "And you'll have your protective eye gear!"

"If the sun ever disappeared the stars would still shine," Mom says.

"Sure, but we'd still depend on the sun's movement. The sun is a star. It's the center of our universe," my sister says. "Which means Kaia's right.... Chaos would ensue. Especially in Hollywood."

"And for sure there'd be zombies," I add.

"Maranhigs! Filipino zombies!" Lainey says, and we bust up again.

Dad slathers on sunscreen. "Considering this bright sun now, I think we'll be okay, girls."

"Don't say we didn't warn you." Lainey shrugs. "All right, who wants to paddle out?"

"Is there any other reason we're here?" Dad says.

Mom pulls out a stack of celebrity magazines. "No thanks, I've got some important reading to do."

"Kai-Kai?" Lainey says.

"Someone needs to stay and bury Toby." I scoop sand and let it slip over his feet. He squeals. Toby's three and definitely a Santos, because he could live at the ocean. Our family loves trying out different beaches all along the coast. We have one we can walk to from home, and we have spots like this, where we drive to and spend the day.

Dad and Lainey grab their boards, run to the shore's edge, jump in, and paddle out until we lose sight of their silhouettes.

Toby's little face scrunches up. "Where's Lainey?"

"She's still there, you just can't see her."

Out in the distance a wave breaks. It swells and gets larger as Lainey and Dad paddle to catch it.

The ocean can scare people because it's unpredictable. Sometimes the waves roll in calm and smooth, but other times they roar. It's tough to know how to face the water. Lainey's told me how big waves make her nervous—normally it's Dad who rides them—but this time she beats him, jumping to a squat on her board before standing tall.

Mom covers her eyes. I hoist Toby onto my shoulders.

The wave looks ginormous. Lainey skims the surface and

water begins to curl over her, rising higher and higher until she's covered.

"A barrel!" I shout.

For a second I lose sight, but then she tunnels right through.

"You can open them now," I say to Mom, and she looks.

Mom clasps her hands. "I can't believe she did it!"

Dad and Lainey paddle back in, out of breath. We run up to them.

"Did you see that? My daughter's first tube!" Dad shouts to random people on the beach, and he and Lainey erupt into laughter. "How'd it feel?"

"Scary . . . but only at first." Lainey's like Tatang—always doing what they set out to do.

They lay down their boards and are drying off when I notice Mom crying.

"Are you okay?" Lainey asks.

Mom shakes her head but smiles through happy tears. "I had this memory of you playing here when you were little. . . . And now you're so grown-up." They wrap their arms around each other. Toby jumps up and Dad swings him in circles.

I see sunshine everywhere I turn.

• • •

We had a full day, the kind that lingers with the citrusy smell of sunscreen even after I've taken a shower. I pull a brush through my wet black hair, trying to untangle the knots, when the sound of giddy chatter reaches my room. Tatang and Lainey.

I sneak to Lainey's door, which is opened a crack. I flatten my back to the wall and scooch in to listen.

"Finally you'll see our beautiful home country, Elena."

"You have to show me *everything*, Tatang. I want to see where you grew up, all the beaches, I want to ride a jeepney, and I definitely want to shop the huge malls in Manila...."

Tatang's got a busy summer ahead. In a few days he's going to visit his sister in Hawaii. After he gets home we'll have some time together, but then he'll leave *again* for his yearly vacation to the Philippines. Lainey's lucky because they'll get to meet up there—she's joining him at the tail end of her trip, and he's planned a fun to-do list: meeting distant family, surfing, and doing tons of sightseeing. He'll make the best tour guide.

I wish I could see the Philippines with him, too.

"Elena, you amaze me with your accomplishments," says Tatang.

That's all my family's talking about lately. Toby's the cute one and Lainey's the smart one, but I haven't figured out what I'm good at yet.

For a second I catch a glimpse of Lainey and Tatang and my eyes meet theirs.

I step back.

"Kaia?" Lainey says.

"Come in and join us, my dear," Tatang says, but I run to

my room, shut the door, and sit at my vanity. As soon as I do, there's a knock.

"FBI, open up!" the voice says. When I don't respond, Lainey asks, "Can I please come in?"

"I guess."

"Hey, you." She hops onto my bed and tries to meet my gaze, but I'm too embarrassed.

I stack some tiny pots of eye shadow, still in their boxes. Lainey gave them to me as a goodbye present even though she's the one leaving. My sister loves giving me little surprises and she knows exactly which colors I'll love—silvery shades and ocean tones.

"Okay, it's just us now. What's up?" she says. Somehow she always knows.

"I tried really hard to get straight As last year." If I could take language arts and history and drawing classes all day I'd be giving valedictorian speeches too, but algebra trips me up every time.

"It's not an easy thing, is it," she says.

"But it's easy for you."

Lainey comes over and kneels so we're eye level.

"You know what's not easy for me? Drawing things so realistic they look like they'll leap off the page. Using colors to paint a story on someone's face. Making friends. You want me to go on about your talents? I can, you know. The whole night."

Finally I look at her. "I'm not great yet with the makeup art."

She grabs a pot of a glittery shade and throws it at me. I catch it.

"Then *get* great. Practice. That's what I had to do to get straight As."

I have this newish hobby: makeup effects. I read about it in our school library and Lainey let me dig through her makeup drawer to experiment. Now I'm hooked.

Tatang never brags about me the way he does about Lainey.

Maybe this is my summer to change that.

2

I sit at my vanity with jars of brushes and sponges and a tray of little pots of eye shadows, spread out in a sea of different colors. Today I'm learning a new technique: the ombré effect. That means blending light to dark, or dark to light.

Lainey and Tatang have both been gone for nearly two weeks, and I can't wait for them to see how much better I've gotten.

I press a stencil of fish scales to my cheek, dip a triangle sponge into a shade called Shiny Shamrock, and dab it over the scalloped pattern so that my tan skin warms the green. I do the same thing along my temples and forehead in Misty Aqua. My dark eyes shine against the bright colors.

Last year a few girls in sixth grade started wearing lipstick and blush to school. My parents wouldn't let me do that even if I wanted to. But they don't mind this kind of makeup. It's more like art.

When I was a little kid, whenever someone asked "What do you want to be when you grow up, Kaia?" I always had a different answer:

An artist like Dad. I'm not as good, but I've always loved to draw.

A chocolate-cake tester—someone who eats chocolate cake for a living. I don't know if this actually exists, but it would be the world's best job if it did.

A Sirena. A Filipina mermaid. Part human and part sea creature, a beautiful and powerful guardian of the ocean.

I know now I can't be a real live mermaid, but it turns out I can transform anyone into a fanciful creature with a pop of color and my imagination.

Dad works as a digital effects artist at a movie studio, and there's a whole department there for special-effects makeup. That's a job I want one day. I've been using different characters from Tatang's old tales to practice.

I apply the final dusting of glitter with a fat brush. Sunshine pours in and makes my cheeks shimmer.

Not bad.

"Kaia! Kaia Santos!" a voice shouts from outside. I run to the window. Trey leans on his bike, grinning and waving. "Kaaaaiiiiiaaaaaa Santoooooooos!"

"Want to come up?" I yell back. "I'm mermaiding!"

Trey looks both ways and jets across the street. Then, his usual entrance: the doorbell ringing twice, a quick hi to Mom, his footsteps galloping up the stairs to my door, which flies open.

"Let me see." Trey throws himself onto the bed and I jump up next to him. He flashes the biggest smile. "Awesome."

"Glad you like it, because you're up next."

Trey lets me test out different looks on him. He doesn't normally wear makeup, but he's used to wearing it for theater productions, and maybe he'll put on the occasional guy-liner for fancy occasions. He wants to act one day. Both of his parents are pharmacists, and at first they didn't want Trey to love acting so much—they wanted him to be into *their* hobbies—but now it's his dad who starts every standing ovation at Trey's plays. Sometimes Trey gets to skip classes to go on auditions, which happens a lot at our middle school since everyone in LA wants to be famous (even our plumber, says Dad). Trey's a natural. He can cry on cue without eye drops.

I pull up a chair and throw him a leg from a bright blue fishnet stocking I've cut up. He yanks it over his head so that it covers his face. The holes act like a stencil, and they make a crisscross pattern against Trey's dark skin. He looks like some kind of weird performance art.

"Name your look: Glitter Dots, Magical Merman, or Merman Zombie?" I say.

"Hmmm...Hint of Merman."

I give him the jar of brushes to hold while I work my magic. When I'm done I peel the stocking off and admire the result: a soft pattern of diamonds blending into his cheek like they're part of him.

"Reveal time!" I reach for Dad's old Polaroid camera and point it to face us, and we give our best mermaid grins.

Click!

The camera spits out a square. Trey grabs it and waves it around to air-dry.

"Gimme!" I yank it away and we hunch over the image.

Us, only shinier.

I search my wall for an open space in the growing mass of practice photos. My gaze lands on one of Mom and Lainey made up as mystical engkantos, Philippine nature spirits who live in seas and rivers and forests and can bring good or bad luck. We did this one right before Lainey left. I really miss her. Lainey gets me. Trey and our other best friend, Abby, wish they had a big sister like mine.

Trey glances at his phone. "Hey, Abby's at the Promenade. Want to go find her?"

"But we've never gone out in public like this."

"So? We'll be the coolest merpeople on land!"

He's right. If I'm going to become famous at this I need to start showing more people my art.

"Sure, let's go ask my mom."

Trey holds up the picture. I tear off some tape and pat it into place on my wall, trying to make it stick.

● ● ●

Downstairs we find one of my favorite people.

"Uncle Roy!" I shout.

"Kaia de la playa!" he shouts back.

Kaia of the beach.

My uncle has lots of nicknames for me, and that's my favorite.

Kaia is a Hawaiian word for "sea." My parents honeymooned in Hawaii. Elena, my sister's name, means "shining light" or "bright one." We're their sun and their sea. They tried to name Toby something oceany too, but they couldn't agree on something they liked.

I run up to hug Uncle and he pretends to fall down. "Ugh! You're like a linebacker now!" he says. "Trey! My favorite thespian!" They fist bump.

"We didn't hear you come in," I say.

Uncle Roy studies my face. "Ooh…nice colors!"

I have my list of things I want to be when I grow up; Uncle Roy's still working on his. He goes to culinary school while teaching yoga and selling condos. Sometimes people think he's an actor because of his striking face, strong biceps, and huge brown eyes.

Uncle likes to take me to new restaurants, and he says to the waiters, "Bring the dessert first, please." We *always* order dessert first.

He's Mom's little brother, a bachelor with no kids. Dad's family lives up in Sacramento, a six-hour drive away, so I don't see them as much as Mom's side.

Of all my family, maybe except Tatang, Uncle Roy is the most relaxed. He's so patient that last Christmas, when one of the aunties poked his belly and said, "Maybe it's time to start laying off the bibingka cakes, Roy?" instead of getting offended he said, "I think my cute pooch makes me pretty guapo." Handsome. Then he stood up and made his stomach protrude like he'd swallowed a bowling ball. My cousins and I burst into giggles and he whispered to me: "Gratitude is my attitude."

It's also why sometimes he goes to Palm Springs with his friends for the holidays.

Tonight Uncle's babysitting Toby because Mom, Dad, and I are picking Tatang up from the airport. I'm sure Tatang will come back with a new Hawaiian shirt—he owns one for every occasion.

"You ready for Big T's return?" Uncle asks.

I point to our chalkboard wall. "I present to you the Epic To-Do List of All Phenomenal Things! It's everything Tatang and I are going to do this summer." Hopefully he likes tandem biking, movies at theaters with luxury recliners, and viewing the eclipse.

A trail of teeny-tiny black ants creeps up the chalkboard wall. I place my finger near one and it crawls onto my nail. I study its frantic movement, then gently set it down. Most people would clean them up, but not my family. Ants parading around in your home bring good luck, so I know Mom is letting them be for Tatang's return.

Right now she's puttering about and sweeping the floor with her walis tambo, a broom with long, wispy bristles fanned out. Mom wipes her brow. "Okay, guys, I think the house is all set for a prosperous arrival."

"Mrs. Santos, would you like any help?" Trey asks.

Uh-oh. If we don't make our escape now, we'll get stuck here and I won't have any time to see Abby.

"Why, I'd love some help, sweetie, thank you," Mom says.

"Should I open all the windows?" he asks.

I do a facepalm. "Mom, may we please go to the Promenade?"

I'm too late.

"Trey," Mom says, "opening windows is for *New Year's*, so we can let in all the good luck." She hands Trey a bowl. "Go into the kitchen and load this with ten of the shiniest round fruits you can find. That'll help fill the house with prosperity."

"You got it!" He marches out and Mom follows.

My family does things that a lot of other families don't— Filipino things.

Mom never cleans the floor with her walis at night because she doesn't want to sweep away any wealth. On New Year's Eve we turn on all the lights to make sure the coming year is bright. And Lainey always eats only the top of the rice, so she can be at the top of her class. Mom and Dad say their parents made them do all of these same rituals, so it's one way to honor them. I like that.

Trey and Mom return with the bowl full of waxy red apples.

"You kids hungry? I'll make you a snack," Mom says.

"Mom? Promenade?" I say.

"Please?" Trey says.

"Pretty please?" Uncle Roy says, batting his lashes in an

exaggerated way, and Trey and I do the same until she has no choice.

"You have two hours, young lady. I don't want to hit traffic on our way to the airport."

"Thanks!" Trey and I shout as we dash for the door.

Outside, we snap on our helmets, I slap my skateboard onto the pavement, and we roll.

3

Summer greets us everywhere we turn and the sun warms me like a hug. Joggers and walkers pass, then people on scooters and bikes. Everyone is wearing sunglasses and flip-flops, sipping smoothies and looking like one big health food ad.

Everyone's heading west—to the beach.

When I was little, I learned directions by remembering that west means water. The "two Ws." It's hard for me to get lost in LA because I always know that home means near the ocean.

Dad likes to gloat that we've made everyone's weekend thing our everyday thing. The perfect weather forces people outdoors to do beachy stuff, even in winter.

We live in Santa Monica, a part of LA, but I have uncles and aunties and cousins and lolos and lolas all over Southern California. Mom's parents are from the Philippines, and she was born here. Dad's parents are from the Philippines, but he was born there and came here as a baby. Mom taught me that a lot of Filipinos immigrated to California in the 1960s, like Tatang and Nanang Cora, my great-grandma, because of a law that brought in nurses like Nanang. During those days a movie ticket cost a buck and a chocolate bar was five cents—what a deal.

My great-grandparents had a hard life at first, but now we have a good one because of them. Tatang and Nanang had one dream: to put their children through college. They worked three jobs each, and it sure wasn't easy. When they arrived no one in their new country would hire Tatang as a teacher, even though he had a degree and had taught in the Philippines.

He says, "I guess they didn't know what to make of me."

He took the only job he could get, as a janitor at a high school, where the kids called him mean names. It made him question why he left behind everything he knew. But Tatang stayed positive. The principal helped him get a job teaching middle school. When he finally retired, the school threw him a huge celebration, because he was the most inspiring teacher they'd ever had. Everyone loved him.

"It was never luck, only hard work," he likes to say.

Trey rides ahead of me. "Wait up!" I shout, and we race to a stoplight across from the Third Street Promenade. It's a long, closed-off street three blocks from the ocean lined with shops and cafés. You see every kind of person there: old and young, local and tourist.

Beside us, people carry surfboards on their heads. As the light turns green we cross in a pack.

Trey finds a bike rack and locks up. Some tough-looking guys in black leather jackets nod our way and say, "Cool scales."

"See?" Trey says to me. "They love us."

We walk into the stream of people and street performers until we spot Abby.

"Gabby Abby!" Trey shouts, but she doesn't hear us. She's pointing a camera at a man and a woman belting out songs while people throw money into a guitar case.

We've called our friend Gabby Abby since kindergarten because Abby knows how to talk. She says if she's ever going to be taken seriously as a female film director she needs a big voice that people will listen to. It works for her. Even when Abby blabbers on about things she's clueless about, she does it in a way that makes people think the opposite. Lainey calls this confidence—I could use more of that. We're the best trio, because whenever one of us starts talking, the others' brains fill up with ideas until we're all bursting to do something.

Abby's our own personal friend-ographer. She gets her good eye from her mom, who's also a photographer. I have no idea what her dad does, and neither does Abby, since they've never met.

Abby points her lens at us and we make cornball faces.

"Aww, you guys mermaided without me?" she says.

"Jealous?" Trey teases.

Abby reminds me a little of a mermaid right now in her teal and silver sequined skirt. She loves girlie things.

"What are you doing?" I ask.

"Practicing the rule of thirds." She shows us the singers on her camera screen—they appear way off to the right. "It's more interesting if the thing you're shooting isn't smack dab in the middle of the frame. What do you think?"

"Weird," Trey says, but I nod.

"I like it."

One of the singers makes eye contact with me, but I look the other way. I've seen their act before—inviting people up to sing. I'm a horrible singer and would rather stay behind the scenes, thank you very much. But Trey takes the bait and jumps up to the mic. Strangers clap along as he croons "I Can See Clearly Now."

"Gonna be a briiight... briiight... sunshiny daaaaaay...," Trey belts out, and Abby snaps away. Neither of them cares who's watching. They never get nervous performing in front of strangers the way I do.

My friends are super talented. Last summer Trey played Peter Pan in a community theater production, and Abby won a photography contest—for adults!—at our neighborhood library. She entered the wrong category by mistake and when the library found out she was only eleven, they still gave her first place.

In school plays, I get cast in snoozer roles like "tree stump" or "rock." I always lose the spelling bee on my first word, and I'm not into sports, so I don't have any trophies. And sure, last year in sixth grade our teacher gave me the Perfect Attendance Queen award, but everyone knows that doesn't count.

If I want to be good at something too, then Lainey was right—I need to practice more. If I keep going and find some inspiration to help me get better, I'll finally stand out.

"Earth to Kaia...Earth to Kaia..." Trey pops up by my side.

He stretches his arms and flings them around me. Abby throws hers around his, and soon we're locked and squeezing so tight that we almost topple. We laugh so hard.

"Let's hear it for our special guest," the street performers say, and Trey runs back for a quick bow. Abby and I clap along with the crowd.

"You guys want to come over for dinner?" Abby asks as we cut through the Promenade. Usually dinnertime at Abby's means walking from their apartment to a pizza place on Montana Avenue where she and her mom take pictures of their food before digging in.

"Sure," Trey says.

I shake my head. "Sorry, can't be late to pick up Tatang." I made a really good welcome sign to greet him at the airport.

"Oh, I forgot. I can't wait to hang out with him!" Abby says.

"Let's go. I'm starved," Trey says to Abby.

"See you at camp!" they shout before heading back into the crowd.

It's a clear day, perfect for skateboarding near the water—and finding my spark. I squint at my watch; there's still time.

• • •

With a *whap* I throw my skateboard to the sidewalk and push onto it, weaving in and out of people in a smooth zigzag. To my right stretches miles of sparkly ocean. As a little kid I thought engkantos, the environmental spirits, lived beneath the waves and were what caused the glittery light. Sometimes I still like to believe that.

The ocean is my daily dose of what Uncle Roy calls "mental tranquility." Water calms the soul. That's why people like taking beachside walks and trips to lakes.

I peek up at bright clouds filling the horizon. One day the water in them will turn to rain and flow into rivers and seas until the sun warms it up and the cycle starts again. Tatang likes to say that water's always changing but it still has a beginning and an end.

I skateboard along until the street turns into a steep, narrow lane, so I tuck my board under my arm and walk across the wooden pier.

The entrance has more street performers and people selling stuff, plus rides and games. A super-scary roller coaster looms above.

I spot a table where I see a cat, a lady, and a huge sign:

CHANGE YOUR LIFE WITH PSYCHIC CAT!

The lady is older and wears a purple turban with a matching velvet cape. She seems bored sitting there, filing her nails with a grim expression on her face. No one's stopping to watch her act.

I squeeze between a steady stream of people and read the sign more closely:

Psychic Cat Will Help You:
Face Change!
Focus on the Positive!
Live in the Moment!
Be Happy!
ETC.!!!!!!!!!!

The woman peers up at me. In front of her sits a stack of tarot cards and a curled-up white cat, napping in a sunny spot, wearing its own turban with a fancy feather popping out like an exclamation point.

This cat does not look like a life-changer.

"Is this Psychic Cat?" I ask.

"In the flesh. Meet Frederick."

"May I pet him?"

She shrugs. "If he'll let you."

Frederick's fur feels warm under my touch; he opens his eyes—barely.

"How does Psychic Cat work?"

"Want to know a secret?" She motions me to come closer, then whispers: "He doesn't."

The woman cackles a nutty laugh and claps her hands together.

"So you mean . . . this is false advertising?" I smile, but I'm not really joking. Tatang says always speak your mind.

She taps her head. "You're a smart cookie, I can tell. What I mean is that Frederick, Psychic Cat, does not aid in the way one might expect. But he is certainly an impetus for wonderful, magical things. Psychic Cat gets the *ball rolling*." She circles her pointer fingers around each other.

"I still don't understand."

"People who meet him are able to manifest happiness because they just need a cute kitty as a jump start. But really... it is *they* who help *themselves*."

"How, exactly?"

"Let me show you." She reaches for a deck of cards wider than her palm. "Tell me what you wish for. The one thing in life your heart desires most."

I think about it.

There are so many things, like... a new skateboard, or for my parents to let me watch R-rated movies, or to be taller.

The woman shakes her head, slams her palms onto the table, and says, as if she's read my mind, "No, no, no. If you cannot consider my question more deeply then I cannot help you."

"May I please try again?" I ask, but she shoos me away like a fly.

"No freebies here!"

The woman restacks the cards. Frederick yawns.

Shoot. I should have thought of something better.

A pack of people begins to form around Psychic Cat and the lady starts her act again. I wedge my way through and make my way home.

A busy airport makes me happy because it feels like a place where Very Important Things happen.

My parents and I wait downstairs in baggage claim.

"What about him?" Dad asks, pointing to a guy in a suit sprinting across the floor, his tie flapping.

"He's been away on business but his wife just had the baby. Heading straight for the hospital," I say.

"Nice one," Dad says.

I made up this waiting game of trying to figure out peoples' stories. The airport's a great place to play.

Tatang's flight has landed. Somewhere, he's taxiing on the tarmac, probably telling his seatmates corny jokes. Around us, drivers hold up signs with passengers' last names. I have my own sign. It has a big hole cut out for me to stick my face through and on top I wrote *Who's Excited Tatang's Back?* Red arrows all around the circle point at me.

I poke my head in to practice. "What do you think?"

"You're hard to miss," Dad says, beeping my nose.

Mom checks her phone. "He's almost here."

"What do you think I should do with Tatang first?" I ask.

Mom says, "I don't know, but I'll bet he has something fun up his sleeve too. He was like that when I was a kid."

Tatang is Mom's grandfather. Lolo and Lola, my grandparents—Mom's parents—passed away when I was younger. Luckily I still have Lolo and Lola on my dad's side.

The escalators start to fill with people riding down. First I see their feet, then their legs, and last, their faces. No glimpses of him. I keep searching.

Then—I see a pair of fresh green sneakers, followed by cargo shorts, followed by a bright shirt with an electric-guitar print, topped by a brown wrinkled smiling face and a straw fedora.

At last!

I stick my head through the sign and he spots me.

Tatang points, throws his head back, and laughs. It's one of my favorite sounds because he uses his entire face, body, and soul, and it makes everyone else laugh, too, like a domino effect. Mom calls it pure happiness.

He touches down and we grab him.

"Why were you the last person off?" Mom asks. As if he could have controlled that.

"I needed my grand entrance, of course," he says, hugging my parents. "Thank you, Joy and Edwin, for picking me up. And you, Miss Kaia. Come here."

I hand the sign to Mom and let my great-grandpa give me the perfect embrace.

"I'll get your bags, Tatang," Dad says.

"How was it?" Mom asks him a ton of questions in a combination of English and Ilocano, her family's dialect, while we wait at the baggage carousel.

"There's mine." He points to a small black suitcase and Dad pulls it off the belt.

"That's all you brought for two weeks in Hawaii?" Dad asks.

"A pair of sneakers and flip-flops is all I need." Tatang raises his eyebrows a few times at me. "Okay, family, let's go. I'm tired."

"You want to sit down first?" Mom asks, but he rubs her arm.

"You didn't let me finish, my dear Joy. Since when have you known me to be tired? I surfed North Shore every day.... Look!" He flexes. "I'm tired of *airports*."

My family's Filipino friends say Tatang's a little different from the other manongs, older males of his generation, they know. He's not as traditional. We think he's more of an original.

Tatang charges toward the exit, and he reminds me of Toby in how fast he moves. The lines that cup the corners of Tatang's eyes when he smiles are the only way to tell his age. They mean he's lived a lot.

As we leave, some guy taps Tatang on the shoulder and says, "Nice chatting with you, Celestino!"

My great-grandpa makes friends everywhere he goes.

Large glass doors slide open for us as I take Tatang's hand and we swing. I feel good things ahead.

● ● ●

At home, Dad quietly opens the front door. It's way past Toby's bedtime, but my little brother bursts out of nowhere and runs straight into Tatang's arms.

"We! Got! Cookiiiiiiies!" Toby shouts. Tatang swoops him up and the room fills with giggles.

"Of course you did," Mom says, rolling her eyes at Uncle Roy, who shrugs.

"Nice tan, Big T," Uncle says to Tatang, and they hug. "See you tomorrow. Gotta jet—I'm teaching an early yoga class."

"Okay, Little T. Bedtime," Mom says to Toby. "Maybe you should get some rest too, Tatang."

"Nonsense. What's the fun of going away if I don't get to give my great-grandchildren their presents?" Wherever he goes, he always brings us souvenirs. Lainey does that, too.

Tatang wheels his suitcase into the middle of the room, opens it, and starts digging out shopping bags. Toby and I find little glass containers of real shark teeth, tins of macadamia nuts, jars of pretty miniature seashells, and bright T-shirts that say *Aloha* with shaka hand signs on them.

"Bought this for Elena," Tatang says. He lifts out a sleek digital clock with a touch screen.

"What's that for?" I ask.

"You know how Elena likes to sleep in. I don't want her to be late for her morning classes when she starts college. I'm told this clock is state-of-the-art *and* voice-activated. Very special, right?"

It doesn't seem fair she gets something so cool just because she wants to be a doctor.

Tatang reaches into the suitcase again and this time pulls out a grass skirt that looks Toby-sized. I slip it onto my brother and he runs around the room flapping his arms.

"Actually, anak, the hula skirt's for you," Tatang says.

I make a face. "But that's for little kids."

"Kaia!" Mom gives me her "If you don't have anything nice to say, don't say anything at all" look. "How about a 'thank you,' young lady?"

Mom's right; that was kind of rude. "Sorry, Tatang. Thanks for the presents—I'm glad you're home. That's the best gift." I scoop up some souvenirs to put away, including Lainey's new clock.

He cups my face. "Samesies," he says, which makes me laugh. "I'm so happy to finally spend a bit more time with my Kaia."

"A bit? We have the whole summer! Come on, I have something for you."

Tatang follows me into the kitchen and I show him the chalkboard wall.

"What's this?"

"Everything we're doing together, just the two of us! Like when you make your lists." If Lainey gets to do a bunch of fun things with him in the Philippines, it's only fair that he and I do that here.

He reads every line, nodding. "Not bad, not bad." For the briefest moment, I catch his worried face. Tatang rubs his neck.

Would he rather be hanging out with Lainey? Or doing something else?

"I like what you've put down here, my Kaia. But you know it doesn't matter how we spend our time together. I love any day with you."

Maybe he's tired and jet-lagged. I give him a hug. At least I'll have him all to myself this summer.

● ● ●

Upstairs, the door to Lainey's room is open, tricking me into thinking she's home. I stick my head in but the bed's made, with the sheets tucked in. Lainey's always kept a neat room. Not like mine, where Mom gets mad at the piles on my floor or the sketch pads scattered around. I shove them under my bed whenever she asks me to clean up.

I check my phone. Zero texts from Lainey. Her teachers made a rule of no screen time, which sounds awful. They only get to call once a week, and in between, their teachers email pictures and updates. I wish I could hear her voice right now.

The numbers on Lainey's new clock glow green as I plug it in and set it on her nightstand, next to the framed photo I gave her as a graduation gift—from the first time I tried makeup art. We'd decided that Filipina mermaids had shimmery turquoise cheeks and flowy black curls woven with seaweed ribbons, but I gave us rainbow globs on our faces and knots in our hair. We couldn't stop laughing.

When Lainey finishes college she wants to stay in New York for medical school.

"Won't you get homesick?" I asked.

She shook her head. "Home's not *where* you are, Kai-Kai; it's *who* you are."

I didn't really get what she meant. How do I tell who I am or who I want to be? Some kids, like Trey and Abby, just know. Trey wants to become a famous actor. Abby's going to direct romantic comedies. Lainey's always wanted to be a doctor. Supposedly, the thing you wish to be when you're twelve is the thing of your heart, and your whole life you'll want to grow up to be that one thing, even if you get off track. When I told Uncle Roy I'm into effects makeup, he said it means I'm someone who can help transform people. I like that.

I smooth Lainey's quilt and lie down. Our lola on Dad's side sewed it with blue at the top for sky, tan at the bottom for sand, and a surfboard sticking straight up.

The quiet's not bad, although Lainey's room is going to look and sound even emptier when she starts college. I wonder how that will feel.

Toby runs in and throws himself onto the bed. He pulls me up and we jump as high as we can, trying to touch the ceiling. So much for the silence.

"Higher, Kaia, higher!" he shouts, and we reach up like we're grabbing for stars.

"I thought I heard a ruckus in here," a voice says. Mom stands in the doorway with a big grin. "Is it tickle time?"

"Yep!" Toby says, and now she's on the bed too, arms and legs and laughter all piled up.

"Cooookiiiiies!" Toby says, and he climbs down and skitters out.

"I blame your uncle," Mom says.

We lie on our backs. I sigh.

"What's that for?" she asks.

"I'm never going to see Lainey again, am I?"

"What are you talking about, silly?"

"She's having so much fun on her own, I bet she'll never want to come home now."

Mom sits up, slips a rectangle out of her shirt pocket, and hands it to me. "Will this make you feel better?"

A postcard. The front says *Philippines* with a map of the islands and a background of crystal-clear blue-green ocean.

I flip it over.

Dear Kaia,

It's so different here, but I love it!!!! I'm having the best time. The other kids are really cool. I wish I could stay longer, but I can't keep New York waiting! I also wish you could see the country where Tatang grew up, but one day we'll come back and have sister adventures.

Hey, how's camp? Miss ya.

XOXO,
Lainey

I should feel happy to hear from her, but my eyes sting. It's like Lainey's senior year all over again, when she was so busy with school that I barely saw her.

"You know, Kaia, when Lainey's done with college it'll be your turn to go. Then *I'll* be the sad one."

Mom's frowning now. We stare back up.

"At least Tatang's home," I say.

That cheers me up, until I remember he'll be leaving again to join Lainey. My parents almost didn't let her go—they thought it was too far for her to travel without them for a whole summer—but Tatang convinced them by saying he'd meet Lainey and they'd fly home together. She'll get to see his old village and the bamboo-and-cement house where he was born and raised, and they'll do a daily stroll through green fields that lead them to the ocean.

I've never visited the Philippines. My parents say it's too expensive to travel there right now—plus all of our immediate family's here—but that one day we'll go.

Tatang has lived in California for more than sixty years and says it's his home, but he still calls the Philippines his home too. I've heard his childhood stories enough that his memories have become mine. I can imagine how warm the sea feels and can picture wonders like the terraced rice paddies that climb thousands of feet up mountainsides, and hills that look like chocolate. "We carry a place with us," he likes to say. I think that means your roots stay planted somewhere deep inside you no matter where you live.

Mom checks the time on Lainey's new clock. "Goodness, I didn't realize it was so late. Do me a favor, please, honey, and help Toby brush his teeth while I clean up downstairs?"

I nod and get up to search for my brother.

• • •

Toby and Tatang sit in the backyard under sparkly twinkle lights that hang over the patio. Their faces glow.

"Look, it's your Manang Kaia! Just in time for a tale," Tatang says.

I pull up a chair. Toby runs over and cuddles in my lap.

"We've missed hearing your stories, right, Tobes?"

"Good, because here's a new one. It takes place in the times when the sky lay close to the ground," Tatang says. "There was once a Filipina woman who wore beautiful beads around her neck and the prettiest comb in her hair. One day the woman went outside to pound rice with her mortar and pestle, so she took off her necklace and comb and hung them from the sky. Each time she lifted her pestle, it would strike the sky above. At one point she raised it as high at it would go. It struck the sky so hard that it caused the sky to rise up and up and up until the woman lost all of her ornaments. And that's when the comb became the moon and the beads scattered and became the stars."

Toby peers at our great-grandfather in awe—I've had that feeling more times than I can count.

"How do you know so many stories, Tatang?" I've never asked him this before.

"Some I learned from my family. And some... I made up." He winks at me. "You know, long ago, hunter-gatherers used their stories to pass down news about weather or food or about the sun and the stars. So storytelling has always been a way of life. They help us understand our world and appreciate each other better."

I think I know what he means. I never met Nanang Cora, but when Tatang tells us memories of her struggle to raise their family in a new country, I feel like I know her.

"Okay, Toby, say good night," I tell him.

"Not so fast. I want you both to do something for me first." Tatang points above. "Look up. What do you see?"

I don't think I'll ever get tired of him asking this question.

We tilt our heads back and take in the glittery view.

"I see stars!" yells Toby.

"An ocean of stars!" I shout.

"Now, there's something I want you each to remember. No matter where we are, we all exist under this same sky. Even when we're apart we're still with each other." He looks at me. "Right, anak?"

I crane my neck and take it all in. Seeing how the sky stretches above makes me feel a part of something bigger than myself.

When most kids think of summer camp, they probably imagine kayaks and majestic mountains and kids cannonballing into lakes. I picture palm trees instead of pine trees and computer screens instead of fishing rods.

Welcome to Camp Art Attack.

Camp happens at the high school near our house, and I've gone every summer since first grade with Trey and Abby. It's the kind of place where kids can paint and sing and make things, and no one gets mad if we get messy. Right now we're in a classroom having Morning Meeting. That's when we sit in a circle on squishy beanbag chairs with our teacher, Eliza, and talk about how to Get Stuff Done.

Each kid can choose a different focus, like music, art, or Digital Expressions. This year my friends and I decided on Film Fun. We're in a group of thirty or so soon-to-be seventh graders who like to brainstorm lists of the Top 100 Movies of All Eternity or who can sing every song in every animated Disney film ever made. We get the whole summer to play around with fancy camera equipment and watch movies while eating kettle corn. Regular school should be more like this.

"Okay, Art Attackers, housekeeping time," Eliza says.

Everybody calls our camp teacher Eliza instead of Ms. Rodriguez. She thinks "Ms. Rodriguez" sounds too much like her mom.

Eliza's twenty-three, would like to have a serious boyfriend, and has a master's in film theory. I know all this because she likes to talk about herself. Uncle Roy says that's a very LA trait. She teaches here during summers and the rest of the year works the lowliest job in the movie business—production assistant—making copies of script notes and taking latte and lunch orders. She says sometimes she wishes she could skip that part and jump ahead to producer, but that if you have a big vision you have to work hard for it. I like her style.

Eliza picks up a guitar at her feet, looks wistfully out the window, and strums some chords. She also writes heart-wrenchy songs and plays them at a coffeehouse down the street.

"Love is good... love is bad... love is blind...," she croons suddenly in the saddest, raspiest voice. Abby and I catch each other's eyes and we don't know whether to clap or cry. Mom says women in their twenties usually go through a bad-songwriting phase.

She puts the guitar down and swaps it for a clipboard. Her eyes brighten.

"Ready for some super-exciting news, film buffs?"

Trey leans into his beanbag so he deliberately makes a fart

noise with it, and kids snicker. He thinks if he didn't act, he'd try stand-up comedy. I whack him on the shoulder.

Eliza flips to a sheet of paper, clears her throat, and reads:

"'To the students of Camp Art Attack, it is my pleasure to invite you to enter this year's youth competition of the annual Santa Monica Beach Season Film Festival. We want you to submit all of your beach-themed flicks! This year we've added a bonus category: solar eclipse. In celebration of this once-in-a-lifetime event where the sun goes down in LA, we invite you to share all of your entries having anything to do with summertime sunshine—or the lack of it. We will announce five winning youth films to be premiered at the Beach Season Summer-End Gala. The team for each winning film will receive ten thousand dollars, donated to its arts program; individual participants will receive complimentary enrollment in any of our Fall Youth in Film Conference workshops.'"

"No way!" Trey yells, and a buzz travels the room.

"Hold on, there's more," Eliza says. "'We will accept entries in the youth category with a run time of five minutes or less. The submission deadline is July twenty-ninth. Winners will be announced in early August,' et cetera, et cetera.... Okay, I think that covers it." She looks up from her clipboard. "Who'd like to enter?"

Every arm shoots up—mine first.

I've never won a contest. Maybe now's my chance.

That's it!

If I get the grand prize I'll have something for my family

to fuss over for sure, especially Tatang. My head pings with thoughts.

"Who thinks they have a good idea for what kind of film to submit?" Eliza asks.

More arms in the air. She calls on people.

Callie Schilling thinks we should do some sort of flash mob dance on the pier (not bad!).

Aditya Jones would love to direct an action dramedy that involves surfers who turn into giant whales every ninety-nine years under the solar eclipse.

Dave Conway says, "I heard that there's a red carpet and winners ride to the premiere in a stretch limo!" This gets everyone jabbering.

Eliza laughs. "I'm glad you're all on board. Okay, then, Art Attackers, form your groups... and get to it!"

• • •

During lunch, Trey, Abby, and I find our favorite shady spot in the courtyard. We've brought all of our favorites: sandwiches, strawberries, popcorn, Spam musubi, gummy bears, chips, pink donuts (with sprinkles, of course), and avocado sushi. We share everything.

The three of us have always gone to the same school, so we've known each other for more than half of our lives. Supposedly, if a friendship lasts for seven years, it'll last a lifetime. We're connected forever now.

I met Abby and Trey on our first day of preschool. After my parents left, I wouldn't stop crying, so Abby and Trey took my hands and led me to the puppet show corner. Even then Abby directed us and Trey did most of the voices, like they've always known what they're destined for.

Trey rips into a bag of chips. "We're entering this thing as group, right?"

"Duh. Team Win!" Abby says, popping a berry into her mouth.

"What should our movie be about?" I ask.

"Sci-fi," Abby says. "A dystopian end-of-the-world kind of blockbuster would get us to the top for sure."

"No, I was thinking something more realistic and dramatic and gut-wrenching," says Trey. "I want to do some good ugly-crying on camera."

Oh boy. Here comes the tough part. When it comes to making things together, we can never agree on an idea—at first. In third grade we decided to start our own lemonade stand (we were going to make trillions!). Abby wanted to sell lemonade slushies, Trey wanted to sell actual lemons with googly eyes glued on, and I wanted to sell an experience, which involved a plan to build a Rube Goldberg machine that squeezed the lemon juice into a cup. Our business never happened.

Mom says it's a little like how families work: not everyone has the same opinion, but what matters is how we get to the result.

Abby and Trey start bouncing ideas around. At least we all love this part.

"I've got it," I say. "How about something with a super-scary monster with tons of blood and guts that I can design?"

"Oh yeah, like Creature from the Black Lagoon but maybe with... with a jellyfish... and an earthquake," Trey says. "Jell-quake!" This cracks us up, but Abby's not amused.

"You're forgetting about the contest rules. There's no sun-shine in that idea. What we should do is research first and figure out what does well in the marketplace," Abby says. She knows all the Hollywood lingo.

For once I don't agree with her seriousness—we have to start now.

"Maybe we shouldn't overthink it, Abbs," I say.

"You're right," she says, but by the end of lunch we still haven't come up with anything spectacular.

The bell chimes and it makes me think of fairies whisper-ing. They've thought of everything here.

Kids in clusters march across the quad chanting "Red carpet! Red carpet!" and my stomach does a flip. So much com-petition.

One steely-eyed girl says to me: "My group's ready to win this thing."

• • •

After camp I cut through the backyard to find Dad in The Cave. That's what we call our little transformed garage, one part Dad's office and the other part Kaia's Artistic Lair. We each have a wall lined with a long narrow desk holding all our stuff. Dad's side has computer screens and laptops, and mine has caddies of pens and pencils sorted by color, stacks of sketch pads, four mirrors (one of them lighted), jugs of special powder for making prosthetic molds, and makeup containers galore. We also managed to squeeze in a couch, and maybe one day we'll install a dessert bar, but for now that's just a good solid idea.

The Cave's entrance is a large glass door that folds into itself like an accordion, and on bright days we open it wide to let the sunshine in. Mom has an office on campus, so we're the only ones who ever come in here.

Right now the movie Dad's working on has aliens and spaceships, and his crew's in "crunch time," which means they all work a ton of hours, including on weekends. Dad doesn't seem to mind because he loves fantastical creatures as much as I do. He grew up hearing Filipino folktales from his parents and grandparents, just like I did.

I walk up behind him quietly so I don't disturb his concentration.

"Hey, sweetie," he says without looking my way.

I rest my chin on his shoulder and peek at the monitor. There's a black-and-green 3-D grid on the screen.

It's fun watching Dad turn nothing into *something*, the way he can suddenly fill a blank space with objects that look weighty and real. My favorite effect he's ever done was when he transformed an old home movie of me and Lainey: we were bouncing on her bed and he made the carpet beneath us suddenly melt into a fiery mass of hot lava. I think I get my love for making things from him. Whenever we feel a little down he'll say, "Let's create something! Anything!" And when we do, I feel better almost every time.

"Whatcha building?" I ask.

"Nothing yet, just testing out my new stylus." He holds up a fancy computer pen.

"I think you should make the Aswang!"

"Oh yeah? Remind me again which one that is."

"A Filipino shape-shifter who can be a vampire, a ghoul, or a werebeast. I think Mom was going to put that one in her book."

I creep around the room making scary faces as if I'm the shape-shifter.

Mom's writing about Philippine myths and folklore. A lot of kids I know have never heard of different Filipino mythical creatures because they're not in many books, but Mom will change that.

Dad turns around in his chair. "How was your day, kiddo?"

"I'm going to win a bunch of money for our camp," I say, and his eyes get wide. "Maybe." I tell him all about the film contest. "Cool, huh?"

"Very. What will your movie be about?"

"Ding, ding, ding! That's the question of the day." I plop onto the couch. "Do you ever get stuck when you're brainstorming, Dad?"

"All the time."

He stretches and goes out to the pool, and I follow. When I look over I see our faces reflected on the turquoise water.

"So what do you do when you can't come up with a good idea?"

"The best thing is to just go for it. Take a paintbrush without thinking too hard and start slapping on the effects makeup and see where it leads, how it might inspire you."

"Daaaad," I say. "It's not *that* easy."

"It could be if you jumped right in. *Literally.*"

He rushes at me and I shriek. I know what he's up to— trying to throw me into the pool. Dad's done this to me, my mom, and my sister a million times.

We circle and I dash to the diving board. We close our eyes, take a leap, and jump right in, our clothes still on.

I make a giant splash and land in the deep end, water and bubbles rising around me, sun cutting the surface, water filling the light. That first chilly moment between only me and the water feels perfect.

Underneath, Dad and I wave to each other.

The pool perks me up and the water shimmers with possibilities. That's all I needed.

I swim to the surface and float.

Finally it's the weekend. I open my bedroom window and little dust wispies flit and dance. I blow and watch as they settle.

It's my first full Saturday with Tatang back, and I hope he got some rest so we can get to Doing Things.

First up: Ocean Gardens.

I bolt downstairs to shove breakfast into my mouth—a pandesal roll that Tatang warmed up for me and a glass of milk. Coffee and bread is his go-to meal most mornings. It reminds him of his childhood in the Philippines, when the sun would rise and the village baker would walk past his house with baskets of freshly baked rolls to sell. They're a little bit salty, a little bit sweet.

I barely get a chance to eat because Tatang's waiting by the front door, jangling his keys.

"Ready?"

"Yep!"

I slip into my flip-flops, and on our way out the door Dad shouts, "Say hello to Harold!" I flash him a thumbs-up.

Tatang still drives. He passed a test to renew his license not too long ago and got a perfect score. It takes us only a few minutes to get to the Ocean Gardens Community for Healthy Living where some of his pals live, and we park.

"I don't think they know I'm back yet," he says.

"Then this'll be the best surprise."

Tatang came to live with us when I was little, not long after Nanang Cora passed away. I don't remember Nanang, but in pictures she looks like Mom, with smooth black hair and warm eyes.

I've never known anything but having a great-grandpa at home. A few kids at school have grandparents who live with them, mainly other Asian kids like me.

Tatang thought about moving to Ocean Gardens once. Mom didn't think he should and, somehow, she and Uncle Roy changed his mind. He didn't want to burden us, which is so silly, because I can't picture our house without him.

Sometimes my family hears about lolos and lolas, grandfathers and grandmothers, who move back to the Philippines. Tatang says it's because "roots grow deep." They come to the United States to give a better life to their families but return to the place that's most familiar. Maybe I'd feel the same. If I ever had to leave my home I'd miss it, because what would I do without my family and my friends and the place I know by heart?

We enter the main building and check in at the front desk,

where the staff greets us by our names. Sometimes Lainey and I volunteer here on the weekends.

"They're in the courtyard," I say, spotting familiar faces outside, and they wave us over.

"Aloooooha!" Tatang says, and he puts a few boxes of chocolate-covered macadamia nuts on the table for everyone to share. His buddies crowd around.

"He's back!" some say, and, "Long time no see, Kaia!"

Ocean Gardens looks a little bit like a resort and a little bit like a hospital. It has couches for relaxing and outdoor Parcheesi, but also nurses walking around holding clipboards.

The first time we visited, seeing that most people were old and some were in wheelchairs scared me. But after I got to know everyone I realized it wasn't a scary place. Although it's not always cheery. Our friends get sick and some die, and I see that it can be painful to grow older. I know that's how life works, but still. It's hard to see your friends go through that.

"Kaia, you made it just in time. We're about to celebrate my big day," says Harold, one of Tatang's best friends.

Harold and Tatang met when they realized they took the same walk: through the pier, down the beach, back up again to the bakery for coffee and a morning bun. Sometimes I join them and we get soft serves on the boardwalk, even before we've had lunch.

"Happy birthday, Harold! How old are you now?" I ask.

"Guess."

I don't want to offend him by saying a number way past his age, but I'm not very good at this game. Uncle Roy says plastic surgery in LA has a way of faking everyone out, except I'm pretty sure Harold's never had his cheekbones sculpted or anything.

"Umm... seventy... four?" I say, and everyone hoots.

"You're officially still my favorite person," he tells me.

"No, he's ninety-two. Can you believe it?" says Cynthia, another resident.

"Harold's so old that he remembers when emojis were called hieroglyphics!" Tatang says.

"Celestino, you're so old you can remember when water was free!" Harold says. We all laugh.

Laughter keeps people healthy because it changes us; it physically transforms our bodies. Tatang has routines to keep himself young: hanging out playing cards, taking daily power walks, picking veggies from his garden to eat raw, and laughing—tons.

"How was Hawaii?" Cynthia asks.

"Sunny as ever," Tatang says. He whips out his phone. "Want to see some amazing pictures? Not from my trip—I have some better ones."

He scrolls through Lainey at graduation, red hats being tossed into the air. Lainey and some of her new friends in the Philippines swimming in a crystal-clear ocean, walking through villages of bamboo houses on stilts, and hanging off the side of a colorful jeepney. These were sent to my parents from Lainey's teachers.

"Right now Elena and her group are somewhere in Ilocos Norte, not far from where I grew up."

"A future doctor. You must be over the moon, Celestino," says one of the nurses.

"I'm a very lucky great-grandpa indeed."

"Maybe one day you'll be a doctor, too, Kaia!" Harold pats me on the arm.

I try to smile politely, but secretly I'm annoyed. Why do people love saying that to me?

Two nurses bring out a cake, all lit up.

"Hey, the whole gang's here!" one of the nurses says as she places the cake in front of Harold. Harold turns to me.

"Help me blow?" he asks. "You can have the wish."

First we belt out the "Happy Birthday" song. I close my eyes and wish for the chance to do something big this summer, something Tatang can brag about to all his friends.

Harold and I aim and blow. I wave the smoke away and help pass out plates. Everyone digs in.

"Kaia, honey, come see the new flowers I planted," Cynthia says, and we walk to a nearby garden full of bright blooms. Tatang stays to chat with Harold but keeps glancing over at me, with the same look Uncle Roy has when he's telling Mom something he doesn't want anyone else to know. Weird.

When we join our friends again Harold says to Tatang, "We'll do plenty of walking before you go, Celestino." Everyone wants some of my great-grandpa's time, but I still get first dibs.

• • •

After Ocean Gardens, Tatang and I dive into the weekend things we love: feeding goats at the farmers market, froyo with all the toppings, and a visit to the surf shop to check out the big fish tank with the spiky blowfish. It's going to be easy for us to get through my to-do list.

After a full day we head home. During the drive, Tatang asks, "What do you think of Ocean Gardens, my Kaia?"

"It's nice there. Why?"

"Just curious."

He stays quiet and I can tell his mind's off somewhere—it feels like he's not with me, even though we're sitting side by side. We reach a stoplight.

"You remember how I've told you and Elena that I've dreamed of retiring to someplace less busy?"

"Yeah, but if you did you wouldn't see spectacular things like that." I point to one of our favorite characters at the beach: a man wearing a glittery American flag top hat and shades shaped like stars, walking on stilts while holding a giant silver boom box on his shoulder. It thumps out beats.

"Big T!" The guy points to Tatang as he wobbles across the street, and Tatang waves back.

Tatang knows every character around here. He thinks people should introduce themselves to the neighborhood folks they see every day, like the gas station lady, the librarian, the coffee shop barista. It's how he has so many friends.

"Tatang, what were you and Harold talking about earlier?"

"Summer plans. I have some good news."

"What?" I ask.

"Let's get back to the house first. I'm saving it for Share Bears," he says, not looking my way.

"Oh, come on, tell me!" I say, but he shakes his head, smiling. Once Tatang makes up his mind about something, he doesn't budge, so I leave it alone. We rest our elbows out the windows and enjoy the breeze.

7

When we get home for dinner, Uncle Roy's at the kitchen island pulling cartons of Chinese food and fortune cookies from a large paper bag. Each week we try to have one meal with all of us here, even if it's only takeout.

I help my uncle set the patio table in the backyard. Soon we're joined by Mom, Dad, and Tatang, who helps Toby into his booster chair. We sit and pass the cartons in a circle, helping ourselves.

"Okay, gang... Share Bears!" Mom sings out.

When Lainey got so busy during senior year, Mom made up this icebreaker where we have to go around and say one thing about our week—good, bad, anything.

I drum my chopsticks on the table. For once I have something exciting to tell them.

"I'll go first," says Uncle Roy. "I learned how to make caul fat taste good."

We all stare back: *What are you talking about?*

"It's this thin membrane that surrounds internal animal

organs that can be used for baking. Trust me, it's much better than it sounds." I give Uncle my "eww" face and he cracks up. "Next!"

Dad says, "Today's lunch special at the studio was fried crickets."

"For that new bug attack movie coming out?" I ask, and he nods.

"What do they taste like?" Mom asks.

"Crunchy … with a kick!"

"And good for protein," I add.

Whenever Dad's work releases a new movie, the studio cafeteria serves themed meals. That sounds way more like fun than work.

"Joy? How about you?" Dad asks.

Mom sits tall in her chair. "I came up with a great idea for my Asian immigration class this quarter. I'd like you to come speak to my students, Tatang. What do you think?"

"I would be honored, anak," he says, without a smile. Seems strange. Normally he'd be so excited at the chance to teach.

"You feeling all right?" Mom asks.

Tatang nods. "How about you, Little T? What are you sharing with us?"

"I like to eat bugs *and* boogers," Toby squeaks out, and Uncle Roy and I clap.

"You want to go next, Tatang?" I ask.

"After you, my dear. I'm saving mine for the grand finale."

I rub my hands together. "We're doing something amazing at camp!" The details spill out of me. Everyone seems excited, but Tatang's staring at his plate.

"Last but not least," I tell him.

Tatang puts down his chopsticks and wipes his mouth. "I have some good news, family. After I make my trip to see Elena and her friends, I won't return to California. I'll be staying in the Philippines."

"For how long?" Mom asks.

"Why, for the remainder of my days, my dear Joy. It's the retirement I should have planned much sooner. I'm moving back home."

"What are you talking about, Tatang?" Uncle Roy says.

"A permanent move, Roy. We've discussed this before."

Mom shakes her head. "Tatang, I don't understand. Who's going to take care of you all the way in the Philippines?"

"It's the perfect time for me." He looks around the table. "I'm not getting any younger, and when the day comes that I do need more help, I won't be a burden. I have enough money to retire well in my home country."

"You're not a burden to us," Dad says.

"Let's give him a chance to explain," Uncle Roy says. "He's thought this through."

"Of course I have—for the last twenty years. I want to die in my homeland."

"Tatang!" Mom says.

"Oh Lord," Uncle Roy says.

Mom stares at Tatang and tears begin to well in her eyes.

"You're… leaving us?" I say.

"It makes sense at this stage in my life. I still have my house back home, and I'll have our friends and family there."

"But we're your family!" I shout.

My hands shake. I can't believe what he's saying.

He looks at Mom and Uncle Roy. "Children, we've talked about this before and you've never changed my mind. I'll make my move in late August. Elena will be able to travel back with her program instead of with me."

"August? You can't be serious. That's not even two months away!" Mom says.

She and Uncle Roy begin to argue. Toby shouts that he has to go to the bathroom. Uncle Roy tells Mom, "It's not your decision." Dad says, "Joy, listen…"

Tatang looks on calmly.

My head fills with questions. "What about my list of stuff for us to do?" I ask. "And what about the eclipse? And—"

He pats my hand and smiles. "We'll still have plenty of quality time before I go. I won't be leaving until after the eclipse, so we won't miss it."

How can he seem so relaxed and sound like everything's okay?

This can't be happening. Lainey will know what to do.

I jump up, run to my bedroom, and slam the door.

Where's my phone?

My room's a mess. I dig under sketchbooks and makeup photos and piles of clothes and finally find it.

I dial Lainey's number, but it only rings and rings.

My big sister's taught me loads of things:

- Sit at whatever table you want because cliques are dumb.

- You might wish you had blond hair, but one day you won't.

- Make friends in real life, not through your phone.

- If you're scared of doing something, it makes sense to try it once.

- When your legs start getting hairy, don't use Dad's razors, because they nick.

- Mean kids are always the most insecure.

- Sometimes things get hard—but they won't always be that way.

Lainey's the one I go to most for questions about friends and school because she always knows what to say and do. Right now I need her advice more than anything—she'd hate this too. She has to hear what's going on so we can figure this out. Tatang's stubborn, but he listens to my sister. We can convince him to change his mind.

I keep trying and trying Lainey's number, but still no answer. This is the worst.

I throw the phone at a pillow and wipe tears from my face. I never thought Tatang would move back to the Philippines, even though other lolos do that. Maybe I haven't done enough for him to stay.

There's a knock at my door.

"May I come in?" Tatang asks. I run to open it and throw my arms around him. "Tatang, you can't go!"

"It's okay, anak...." He leads me back to the bed. "Come, sit with me, my Kaia. I have something for you," he says, patting the mattress. How can he look so calm?

I rest my head on his shoulder and sniffle as he hands me a book. One of his journals. I've seen him jotting in different journals my whole life but I've never asked what he writes about. This one's bound in brown leather, worn and thinning at the edges, the cover soft under my touch.

I'm not sure what to do with it.

"Aren't you going to take a look?" he asks.

A black ribbon holds a page; I peek inside.

SUMMER TO-DO

Visit Hawaii . . . don't forget the souvenirs!

Learn to fly

Ride Pier Pressure

Sunset strolls

Solar eclipse with Kaia

Final arrangements

Pack

I have a horrible thought: Is this one of those lists people make when they're about to die?

"Tatang . . . are you okay? Are you healthy right now? Is that why you're leaving us?"

"Oh, anak, I didn't show you this to scare you. Please, don't let bad notions fill your head. I'm well and healthy."

I let out a huge breath. "I thought this was a bucket list!"

He chuckles. "No, these are simply things I want to accomplish before going home."

"Why are you giving this to me?"

"I'll be giving you and Toby and Lainey all of my journals one day—there's some juicy stuff in there. I was thinking about your list in the kitchen, and I'm giving you this because I want you to see that we'll be spending a lot of time together before I go. I'll be back to visit, of course. But right now, you can help me focus on a proper send-off. You're my best adventure buddy, remember?"

I glance at his list again. *Sunset strolls.* What Harold said at Ocean Gardens makes sense now. *We'll do plenty of walking before you go, Celestino.*

I look him in the eyes, but I've lost all my words.

Tatang pulls me close and for a long moment we sit in silence. He's the only person I can do this with where it doesn't feel weird.

"Why would you want to leave me?" I finally say.

"Oh, Kaia." He looks at me, then rises. "It's almost the golden hour. Go get your jacket, let's take a walk."

That's his answer to everything, but not mine. It'll only remind me he's trying to fit everything in.

"No, thanks."

"Come. I need a good sunset partner."

• • •

It's that hazy time between day and night. We head toward the ocean the way we've done a gazillion times, almost every day of my life, only this time I'm speeding ahead of Tatang instead of walking side by side. My heart's thumping fast.

I want to get this over with, but he says, "Please, let's not rush. Let's watch and listen."

As upset as I am, I know better than to argue when he gets this way.

I let him catch up to me and we walk through our busy

neighborhood. Every time Tatang's gaze meets a stranger's he says things like:

Good afternoon!

Nice day!

Enjoy this beautiful weather!

Sometimes people scowl back—they're the ones who hate unicorns and dessert. But I get it, because I'm scowling too. This mucky cloud in my head doesn't feel good.

I try to slow my breath.

Tatang likes to say that if you look people directly in the eye, even for the briefest second, they can sense it—a connection.

Right now I'm not feeling very connected to him.

We pass a youngish guy wearing headphones and jeans torn at the knees. Tatang says hello but the guy sneers back. Tatang responds with his widest smile. The guy looks confused, but the corners of his mouth lift slightly.

As soon as he's out of sight Tatang says, "It worked!"

All right, so it did. We keep walking and I start to calm down. Tatang's superpower is making everyone feel their best.

"Let's play the noticing game," Tatang says. That's his thing. We have to point out details we might normally not pay attention to. It's not so easy.

We take turns calling out:

Newly chewed pink gum spit out on the sidewalk.

A breeze that makes the hair on my arms stand up.

Waves crashing less than a mile away.

The more I notice what's in front of me, the more his awful

news begins to fade, and by the time we reach the pier my mind doesn't feel so cluttered. Thank goodness.

I hook my arm with Tatang's and we follow the flow of the crowd, like getting pulled into a tide.

"Let's go down to the beach," he suggests. "I need to make a quick pit stop at the bathroom first. Don't go anywhere where I can't see you, okay? Wait for me here at the railing."

He elbows his way into the restroom.

A few feet away I spot Psychic Cat and walk up to the table. The woman smiles without looking at me.

She shuffles her deck. "I knew you would return."

"Ma'am, may I please try once more?"

"Once more at what?"

"The cards. I didn't get to tell you about the thing I want most in life. My heart's desire—you know—all that stuff."

This time we make eye contact: a connection. She's going to help me figure this out.

"This is not something I do for all passersby, but go ahead. Try again."

I know exactly what my heart needs, for sure, one thousand percent. The woman plunks down the card stack and I close my eyes.

"I want my great-grandfather to stay with us forever," I say quietly.

She studies me. "Interesting."

Frederick opens his eyes and I pet him on the soft spot between his ears.

She reaches into the deck, pulls out a lone card, and sets it faceup.

"Ah, the star. A lucky selection."

There's an illustration of a woman kneeling near water with a cloud of light above her head. It reminds me of a Tatang story about Tala, Filipina goddess of the stars. Once during an evening walk when I was much younger, I got scared in the dark, but he pointed to the sky and said, "Tala's using her light to bring us safely home."

"What does it mean?" I ask the woman.

"Cosmic protection. From this point on even your most challenging moments will have meaning and purpose."

"What's it protecting me from?" I ask, but she doesn't answer. "Please, could you pull another card and tell me if my great-grandpa will decide to stay?"

I have so many questions, but the woman calls out: "Psychic Cat! Come and see! Solves all your worries! Ten dollars for one reading!"

People gather and she looks the other way.

Shoot. Who's going to help me now?

• • •

I lean against a railing and scan the sea of people. The pier's packed with surfers and tourists taking pictures; wild screams come from the roller coaster looping above.

After a few minutes Tatang pops up beside me.

He takes my hand. "Sunset time."

We go down to the sand, slip off our shoes, and let our feet sink in.

Not far from the waves we find a spot and sit, watching the water rise tall and rocky before it breaks and rolls smoothly onto shore. I can never count on the ocean to look the same, even though it repeats itself over and over. Maybe that's why I've never been into surfing, even though Dad's always trying to get me out on a board with him.

"You feeling better now that we've gotten some oxygen to our brains, anak?"

He just gave me the worst news—how does he think I feel?

"What will you do in the Philippines without us, Tatang? And what about me? Does that mean you won't be here for my birthday or for eighth grade promotion next year? I know I won't get valedictorian, but don't you want to at least be here long enough to celebrate? And what about—"

"Kaia." His voice is gentle.

"—what about Toby? Don't you want to see him get bigger? He already grows like five inches every day, and what happens if—"

"Kaia!" he says with a force I rarely hear.

I stop. My heart's racing.

"Where are your feet?" he asks.

My heart's still pounding.

"Where are your feet, Kaia?"

It's the question he likes to ask when I get too stuck on things brewing inside. Tatang's all about the moment. *Where are your feet?* tells me how to stay in what's real, what's here, now. Sometimes it works, sometimes it doesn't.

My eyes water and blur the view.

If Tatang leaves me he'll never return. It's fifteen hours in the air to Manila, another flight to his province, hours of bumpy driving down dirt roads to his village by the sea where I'm related to everyone and they all know my name even though we've never met. He has so many memories there and he talks about them all the time—why would he ever come back?

When I don't answer he asks, "My dear, where are your feet?"

I look down, toes dug into sand, still warm from the day's heat.

"I'm right here. On the beach with you."

I'm right here watching the waves break way out, waiting for the sun to set with someone very important to me. After he goes I may never see him again.

My heartbeat quickens. I try to exhale slowly but it's like I can't catch my breath.

I get up and walk toward the ocean, waves splashing in like loud whispers as my toes touch the edge. The water's cool, and a shiver travels through me.

I fix my eyes in the direction of the sun hanging low,

sloshing my feet farther into wet, heavy sand until they're covered. Normally I'm calmed by the ocean, but when I look out it doesn't seem to end. It makes me feel so small.

My face is wet. I wipe the tears away.

Tatang rests his hand on my back.

"You never mentioned anything about this to me," I say in a quiet voice.

"That's why I brought us here, Kaia, to talk. You can ask me any questions." He hands me a tissue to wipe my nose.

"Does Lainey know?"

He nods. "We discussed it before she left."

Of course he shared it with her first. "You told her but not me?" I start crying again. "And is she happy about it?"

"I wanted her to know before she left. Like you, she wasn't happy, but Elena understands—and I think your parents do, too."

"Are you . . . are you leaving because I haven't done any-thing important?" He probably thinks I never will. He has zero reasons to stick around anymore.

Tatang pulls me close. "Oh, my dear, you are my absolute joy, and my move doesn't change that a single bit." He pulls away and looks me in the eye. "Here's what I'm thinking: Next summer you'll come visit. And before that we'll see each other all the time on our screens, too. But right now, we'll enjoy all of our favorite things here, starting with this beautiful sunset."

He keeps talking, but I've stopped listening.

We're surrounded by the golden hour, Tatang's favorite

time of day, when pinks and oranges blend and everything's rimmed in a halo of light.

"Ah, look at that…," he says.

Like the ocean, the sun never stops. It slips away, but it always comes up again and is something we can forever count on. Walking and sunsets are Tatang's favorite things. In the moment when the sun says goodbye, he's still, so I try never to disturb him when he's watching. I have a lot I want to say to him right now, but even though I'm mad at him, I stop myself.

The sun lowers and people clap or take pictures. Usually we do too.

"The Philippines has beautiful sunsets that we'll watch together. What do you think?" he says.

"I think you're being selfish," I snap. How could he do this to me? The smile lines around his eyes disappear. If he feels bad about this, then I'm glad. He should feel guilty. "I want to go home now."

The only thing I notice during our walk back is the silence.

• • •

We walk into the house and Mom looks up from the couch. "Hey, you two. How was your stroll?"

Tatang peers at me and I stare down at the floor. I feel so bad now for saying rude things to him when he was trying to help, but I still feel like screaming. Inside my pockets I ball my hands into fists.

Tatang smiles at Mom, then at me. "We had… a good chat. I think I'm going to read, then turn in early." He plants a kiss on my forehead before going upstairs.

My eyes feel puffy.

"Come here," Mom says, patting the couch. She drapes her arm around me and squeezes. "Lots of changes happening, huh?"

"We have to make him stay," I say. "He has to!" I can't hold it in anymore and start crying again.

"Oh, sweetie," Mom says, rubbing my back until I'm calmer. Then she looks at me. "We can't make anyone do anything, most especially your great-grandpa. I don't want him to leave either, but this was inevitable. He always meant to return one day. Now that I've had some time to think about it, this is what's best, and your Uncle Roy feels the same. We talked while you were out."

"But how can you be so sure?"

She holds her hands together tightly, like she's trying not to let go of something. "I'm not, but Tatang knows what he needs. I trust him."

"He's going to miss out on every good thing."

"I thought about that. But sometimes life shifts, and even though we don't have an explanation for why, we have to go with the flow and find ways to accept it. This is going to be hard, but we have to respect Tatang's wishes. Let's try to be happy for him."

She holds me close and I catch the sweet, light scent of her

sampaguita perfume—Philippine jasmine. Tatang loves telling the story of how the flower grew all around his childhood
house, and on his walks home from school the smell of it sig-
naled he was near.

Whenever Tatang speaks of "home" I know he means the
Philippines. Mom's right. It's his time.

My head keeps pounding, though my hands start to feel
calmer.

"I guess."

"Maybe we can plan a trip to the Philippines next year,"
Mom says. I try to smile at her—she smiles back. "In the mean-
time, I'm planning a big goodbye party. Will you help me with
the menu? We can come up with a theme and the guest list.…"

Mom rattles off more details—she's already over it. I wish
I could feel the same.

This break is the Worst Summer Ever.

It's late, and I toss and turn in bed. I wish there was a way I could convince Tatang not to go.

I pull his journal out from under my pillow. Something pokes up from an edge, but I can't see anything; it's pitch-black outside.

When I was little I was scared of the dark, but I was even more frightened of the bakunawa, thinking he was in the sky somewhere taking all the Earth's light. I'd hide under my covers, not wanting to peek out in case the dragon-like creature flew past my window and decided to snatch me, too.

What would really happen if the sun disappeared? How long would humans survive without it? Some scientists think that might actually happen in another five billion years. Scary. But one of Tatang's favorite lessons he used to teach his students was that humans can adapt. So maybe if the sun disappeared, people would figure out how to live in submarines in warmer parts of the ocean, or else they'd find a new home, like Mars or something.

I reach over and turn on the lamp to see what's sticking out from the journal—a photo. I shake the pages and it slips out along with a few others, snapshots of my family from before I was born.

I see younger versions of Tatang and Nanang with their children, other photos with their grandkids. There's one of Mom and Uncle Roy as cute toddlers eating hot dogs at Disneyland, their brown faces popping out in a sea of non-Filipinos.

My gaze lands on an old black-and-white square of Tatang surrounded by aunties and uncles and lolos and lolas, standing in front of lush mango trees near his home in the Philippines, fields all around. It's bright. Hot and humid. I can tell from the others in the photo who are wearing their summer clothes and tsinelas, or flip-flops. Tatang looks dressed for the opposite weather, in a button-down shirt, slacks, and the shiniest shoes. Back then he didn't have a collection of colorful sneakers.

Tatang likes telling me the story of how hard he worked for his first pair of nice loafers, which he bought at a fancy store in Manila with money from his first teaching job. He got those dressy shoes *and* his first pair of high-tops—in bright red.

I turn the picture over. On the back in his neat handwriting it says:

73

Start new adventure! Make family proud!

This is of him getting ready to leave one country for another.

Nanang and Tatang were scared to start their new life, but they figured it out—and they did it for me, Toby, and Lainey. That's what he always says. Whenever I get nervous about anything at all, he shares the memory of the day he and Nanang left the Philippines. On the plane they squeezed each other's hands and watched the view of the ocean turn into a sea of clouds. Up there he felt small. The world looked so big.

Another picture stands out: it's of a young Tatang in his army uniform, wearing thick boots. He's standing in front of a painted backdrop of trees and staring off somewhere with a solemn look.

Tatang has told me every Filipino monster story he knows, but he's never shared much about his days as a soldier in World War II.

I study the image for a long time. Tatang looks so young and vibrant, with the same determined eyes.

Sometimes I worry about him getting older and the thought creeps in that he won't be around forever.

If going back to his home country is what he wants in his life right now—a man in his nineties—why would I try to stop him, especially after all he's done to give me the best life?

I tuck the photos back into the journal and bring it with me into the dark hallway, where Tatang's snores vibrate. He has a way of filling a space no matter what he's doing. Normally

I hate his snoring—sometimes it keeps me awake—but I'd take that over him saying goodbye.

Kaia, where are your feet?

I try to feel them bare and flat against the carpet, padding downstairs until they reach the ping of cold tile.

When we're outdoors, Tatang and I like to slip our shoes off and let our soles touch the earth—grass, dirt, or cement—trying to connect to something bigger than ourselves.

In the kitchen I flip on more lights, grab an apple, and plant myself on a stool. I leaf through pages of Tatang's precise handwriting before I stop on his to-do list.

My chicken scratches on the chalkboard aren't too different from what he's written. I learned to make lists from him. Figure out what you need, stick to your decision, write it down, get it done. He came to California with only his dreams and made them all happen this way.

Next to my list is Mom's calendar, full of notes. There's one date she's circled in red: *TATANG'S LAST DAY.*

It finally hits me: He's leaving.

He'll fly out on a red-eye and wake up in his homeland. He'll take off his shoes to feel connected to the one place that makes up every part of who he is, and no one's changing his mind, not me, not even Lainey.

My great-grandfather spent his life helping his family and all of his students. Maybe I don't want him to go, but he deserves our help now.

I crunch into my apple and stare at the dark windows; I imagine ocean foam dissolving into sand.

Suddenly I'm grabbing a stick of chalk, scanning Tatang's list, and mixing his to-dos with mine on the wall. And not the boring ones like "Pack," but ones like "Take many sunset strolls" and definitely "Watch solar eclipse." If he wants a proper send-off that's what he'll get. We'll start with this list.

I'll have to break the news to Trey and Abby about Tatang leaving. They'll be sad too, but at least we'll have the film contest to keep us busy. All we need now is a good idea for it. But what?

Tatang's journal has a chunk of empty pages. I take a pen and start drawing whatever pops into my head—Dad calls this "stream of consciousness," when you doodle or write the first thing that you think of. Sometimes we do it together. Right now I have monsters on my mind—Filipino ones, from Tatang's stories. All my favorite characters are from the tales Tatang likes to tell me whenever I need cheering up.

First I sketch the bakunawa with slithering curves and mischievous eyes, gliding through the sky past suns and moons. He has a rascally smile on his face. I also sketch the siyokoy, part man and part fish; a sirena, a Filipina mermaid; and the tiyanak, a Philippine vampire that takes on the form of the cutest little baby, who cries in the jungle to attract gullible travelers before eating them.

A whole hour later I've filled in a few blank pages.

Hmmm.

I'll give Tatang what he wants—a spectacular send-off—by making *him* proud of *me*. I'm about to start my own adventure.

And there's the spark I needed. Thank you, Psychic Cat, for getting the ball rolling.

I have one last thing to add to my list. In big, bold letters I write:

Win Beach Season.

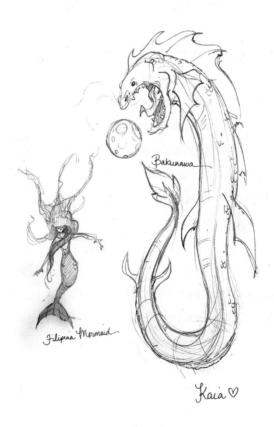

Bakunawa

Filipina Mermaid

Kaia ♡

•••

Upstairs a thin sliver of light cuts under Tatang's bedroom door. It's open slightly, so I push it in.

He's sitting on the bed, his back to me.

"You're up too?" I say. He doesn't reply. "You need anything? Some water?"

Silence. Then I realize Tatang is meditating, hands on his knees, palms up, receiving peace. I try to tiptoe out but he grabs my arm and yanks me near.

"Like this," he says, going back into his pose.

Meditation is all about awareness. I copy him and try to focus on sounds coming through the window—a dog barking, music from a car driving by. But my thoughts scatter: How many new Hawaiian shirts did Tatang bring back? What time is it where Lainey is? Can my friends and I really make a movie good enough to get into the film festival?

That's the hard part about meditating: not letting your mind wander.

He clasps his hands into his lap and turns to me. "How'd you do?"

"Tatang..." I have trouble finding my words, but I know my great-grandpa deserves to hear this. "I'm sorry for earlier. I said some mean things, but I was mad at your news, not at you."

"I know, anak. Are you still feeling that way?"

"Not as much." Luckily. "But... yeah."

He points to the window. "I can barely see the moon. The bakunawa's been busy—and hungry."

He's right. Tonight the moon's thin.

The first time I heard Tatang's bakunawa story was from under a fort blanket with all the lights off except for a flashlight.

"What's the scariest Filipino monster that ever existed?" Lainey asked him then.

"Let me think about this one," Tatang said. "Okay, ladies, one moment."

He turned slowly so we could see only his back, but he whipped around, flicked the flashlight on under his chin, pulled out his dentures, and gave us his scariest monster face.

"This one!" he shouted.

My sister and I screamed and howled.

"What's going on in there?" Mom asked through the door, but that only made us holler more.

Lainey and I won't have any time with just the three of us before Tatang leaves. I hadn't thought of that.

My gaze goes from the window to the wall in front of me, where Tatang's life hangs in little wooden frames: Nanang in a white nursing uniform on her first day of work in a new country. My parents on their wedding day, barefoot on a beach in Hawaii surrounded by their closest friends and family. Mom next to a giant bear sculpture on campus on her first day teaching college—so young, like a student herself.

There are more recent pictures, too: the sweetest, teeniest Toby wearing a fuzzy hat with ears the day he was born, and one of me and Lainey at the top of Griffith Park Observatory with the Hollywood sign behind us. Tatang brought us there, but he's not in the picture because he snapped the shot.

"Do you already have your plane tickets?" I ask.

He nods. "I have so much to do... organizing, packing, saying my see-you-soons...," he says. "Anyway, it's late, anak. Get to bed before the sun comes up."

Tatang's wall of photos stares at me, so many of his happiest moments spread out like a time line. And I notice something else: none of these pictures has him in them, just the people he loves. He's spent his whole life taking care of us.

I focus on my feet tapping the carpet. "Tatang ... I don't want you to go... but I know it's your time," I say softly.

Our eyes meet. His shine. "You are quite remarkable, my dear."

The sadness in my chest feels lighter. His words give me a boost, and suddenly all I can think about is the goodbye gift I'll give him when we win that contest.

Get started. Now.

10

Trey, Abby, and I sit in the courtyard at camp during lunch next to a fairy-tale jacaranda tree covered in fluffy lavender blooms. These trees aren't from LA, they were planted for their beauty. I always think of them the way I think of Tatang—that they came from someplace else but now they belong here.

We lay out our snacks to share and I unpack a purple cupcake from my lunch bag. Ube-flavored—Filipino purple yam. Uncle baked it. He wants to add Filipino flavors to more desserts, and I love this one the most. He says ube is sweet, rich, and unique, a little like our family.

Trey grabs the hand sanitizer hanging from his backpack and douses his palms. He's always careful about germs.

His eyes light up. "Is that what I think it is? Can I have a bite?"

I wave the ube cupcake in front of his face to tantalize his taste buds. "Not yet."

"Guys, some concentration, please?" Abby says. She's

wearing a red bandana to hold her hair back, a T-shirt, and jeans. Her bandana reminds me of a poster in her room that says *We Can Do It!* It's the World War II image of Rosie the Riveter, the woman who could take on any man's job. Abby also has a pencil tucked behind her ear, her favorite look for keeping us on task.

Abby puts a large sheet of poster board onto an easel. She starts writing and crossing things off. Three other boards full of scribbled-out ideas lie on the ground.

Trey and Abby brainstorm while I nibble on the cupcake and wonder: How am I going to tell them about Tatang?

"Okay, crew, let's start from the top and see if we can pick one," Abby says, reading down our list:

- On the morning of the brightest sun, a giant mutant robot piranha terrorizes all seventh graders on Earth, starting with an unsuspecting middle school in Santa Monica. It's *Jaws* meets middle school… only not a shark!!!!!

- A thirteen-year-old diver discovers gold treasure beneath the sea, but the treasure's haunted—and now he's being hunted!!!!!

- A group of half-kids, half-birds crashes onto a tropical island, where they must survive with only a harmonica, a banjo, a bag of gummy worms… and a kid-bird-eating alien octopus!!!!!

Abby caps her pen and taps it to her lips. She's a Libra, so her star sign is the scales; she likes to weigh things out before she makes a decision. It can take her days to decide on something, like what book to write a report on or what funny thing to say in the video birthday card we make Trey each year.

I cross my fingers behind my back. *Please don't take forever on this.*

"Ready ... feedback ... and go!" Abby yells.

"No, no, and no," Trey says.

"Specifics, please," Abby says.

"There's no 'wow' factor." When Trey says *wow*, he holds up three fingers on each hand in front of his mouth so that his fingers form Ws and his mouth forms an O. He's a Taurus. Heart in the right place but doesn't mind arguing.

"Then what *would* wow everyone?" Abby asks.

"Beats me," he says.

"You can't say you don't like our pitches but then not give other suggestions. That's the first rule of artistic criticism. Give me something I can work with, something concrete." Abby folds her arms. I'm glad she's taking this seriously; that will lead us to snagging one of the festival spots.

Trey rolls his eyes. "I did give suggestions, but you crossed them all off!"

"Kaia? A little help here? Don't tell me you hate all of these too," she says.

"No, it's just that ... something happened at home." I tell them about Tatang.

"Are you kidding?" Trey says.

"Oh, Kaia, that's the worst news. No wonder you're so quiet!" Abby sniffles and hugs me tight, which makes me tear up.

"Should we work on this later?" Trey asks.

"No," I say. "Wait." I wipe my face, then rifle through my backpack to dig out Tatang's journal.

"I have something to help... a little spark," I say. "For inspiration."

I flip open to the pages of my Filipino monster sketches and we huddle. Trey jumps up and shakes me by the shoulders. "Kaia, you've been holding out on us!"

"Yeah, this is fresh—Filipino fresh!" Abby says.

I've never gotten this kind of reaction to my work. I used to get in trouble at school for doodling in the homework margins.

I blush. "Abby, you read my mind! I was thinking we could put a Filipino spin on our movie. Hollywood only makes boring monsters that everyone already knows, but this could make it different. If we get into the festival, it would mean so much to Tatang. I want to give him a win as a going-away gift."

Now I cross four fingers behind my back.

"You mean when we get into the festival," Abby says.

"Yes!" Trey punches his fist into the air. "Win it for Tatang!"

"Which creature should we go with?" Abby asks, going into director mode. "Hit me with your best elevator pitch."

"How about ... a bakunawa causes an eclipse, leaving an unsuspecting middle school in total darkness?" I say.

I explain the legend of the sea serpent who eats all the suns and moons until villagers chase him away by clanging on pots, pans, and drums. "There are different versions of this story in other countries, too, not just the Philippines. Neat, huh?"

"Did you say the *vacunawa*?" Abby asks.

I split my ube cupcake and hand half of it to Trey. He stuffs it into his mouth and his cheeks puff out.

"No, it's *B*, for *bakunawa*." I pronounce it slowly for them. *Bah-coo-nah-wah.*

Abby's eyes get big. "I've totally got it! How about a *modern-day* bakunawa story?"

"I totally *don't* get it," Trey says. "What does that even mean?" Little purple crumbs spray out of his mouth. Before I can stop him he grabs *my* half and chomps.

"Hey!" I say. He hands me what's left—one bite—and laughs.

Trey does this kind of thing a lot. Our moms say it's because we're like brother and sister. He's family, but it doesn't mean he can take without asking.

"A modern retelling is when you set an old story to today's times," Abby says.

"Yeah, like movies about Shakespeare but with high-schoolers speaking regular English," I say.

Trey digs into my lunch bag and I swat his hand away.

"Wait a second. . . ." I look at Trey, his mouth still full. "*B* is also for *bully*!" He shoots me a scowl, but I jump in and we start sharing ideas. It's my favorite part of brainstorming—when one thought explodes into another then another, like popcorn popping.

"I love it, Kaia! It'll be the ultimate coming-of-age sci-fi postapocalyptic dramedy!" Abby says. We're quiet; then we all bust up so hard. Now I'm crying from laughing. I wipe my eyes and say:

"Okay, okay . . . We need to win this for Tatang. I don't want him to leave without seeing me do something super special—you know, like how both of you do cool things all the time." It feels good that I can be honest with them. We get each other.

"Stop that," Abby says. "You're already the coolest."

"You know what I mean."

She smiles. "This is for Tatang."

We use the rest of our time to sketch and make lists. I'm screenwriter, storyboarder, and head of effects makeup. Trey will star; Abby will direct. We'll cast some campmates in the minor roles and recruit some onto our production crew. Our movie will take home one of the ten-thousand-dollar jackpots, and we'll give Tatang the most fabulous, impressive send-off—on a red carpet.

Abby says, "Girl, you and me, we'll start our own production company one day." We slap palms.

"I can't wait to play a villain. Evil!" Trey throws his head back with a loud cackle that makes all the other groups look our way.

• • •

When the class gathers to announce our plans I feel a thrill in the room. My hands tingle, like I've captured a secret.

"Okay, gang, quiet down," Eliza says. "Remember, we're here to help each other. You have your core groups, but feel free to use your classmates as crew and talent and work together, especially because the grand prize goes directly into our program. Collaborating gives you an advantage because you're all so amazingly talented!" She flings her arms out. "Now, who'd like to go first?"

Trey shoots his hand up but Abby pushes it down. "Save the best for last," she whispers, and I nod.

Dave Conway and his group go to the front of the room and explain their 1980s period piece about break dancing lifeguards.

"It's going to be a music video with an original score that I'm recording on my tuba," Dave says. Everyone laughs; it sounds pretty fun. They describe each member's job. Dave will direct and be in charge of craft services. (An important job: snacks.)

After each group finishes Trey raises his hand to volunteer, but Abby keeps pulling it down until we're the last ones.

Eliza waves us up. "Last but not least, Team Kaia, Abby, and Trey."

Once we figured out our story line, I drew some large images to help our presentation. We set them up on easels and the room goes silent.

I begin.

"Picture this. The most magical, enchanting Filipino sea creature to ever exist: the bakunawa." Trey and Abby point to a poster board of my sketches and the class oohs and aahs. Eliza leans in.

First I explain the version Tatang loves about the bakunawa being so intrigued by the beauty of the seven moons that he gobbles them up and causes an eclipse.

My voice shakes. That always happens when I have to speak in front of a group. Trey and Abby never seem to get nervous in front of others, but I can't help getting jittery when all eyes are on me.

I pause. What do I say next?

"We're giving an old tale a middle-school spin," Abby jumps in. "The bakunawa is the newest student at The Summer Baking Institute of Magical Sweets. He makes friends with the other student creatures there—the Siyokoy, the Sirena, and the Tiyanak." Trey holds up more of my drawings. "They're baking moon cakes for a class project, but little do they know that their delicious creations are about to disappear."

"That's when . . . ," Trey says in his most dramatic voice, ". . . the bullying begins. Dun-dun-dun!"

"We're not going to spoil the rest," Abby says.

"Wonderful! Feels like a classic creature feature to me. Part mayhem, part destruction, with a touch of magic," says Eliza.

Trey points his thumb at our teacher. "Exactly. What she said."

"Any filmmakers have questions or comments for this group?" Eliza asks.

A hand goes up. Dave Conway's.

"Isn't that a *lunar* eclipse you're describing and not a *solar* eclipse?" He smirks at us.

"Uh, yeah. Why?" says Trey.

"We're having a solar eclipse this summer. *Solar*. It's called the *Beach* Season contest, not *Moon* Season."

"It's still a summery beach story. And actually, our main character's baking sun cakes, not moon cakes," I say. "The cakes are just symbolic."

"Good thinking," Abby whispers.

"Symbolically cringey," someone says, disguised as a cough. I glance around. Some kids can be so rude.

"That's enough," Eliza says. "If I hear that kind of mean-spirited talk then no one gets to enter. Remember, we're in this together. Group Bakunawa, go on. I'm loving your inventiveness."

The class pelts us with tough questions: What will the costumes and makeup look like? Will it have dialogue? Does the creature have a language of its own? Why a lunar eclipse instead of a solar eclipse?

My head rattles. None of the other groups got grilled. If they don't believe in this idea now, what if it's not strong enough to get us to the top?

Abby says into my ear: "We got this."

11

The very next day at camp, Team Bakunawa dives into the thick of preproduction. I love this part, turning nothing into something when everyone's thinking up their best ideas and the energy spreads. I picture lightbulbs on top of people's heads glowing brighter and brighter until—*ding ding ding!*—"Aha!"

Where *do* ideas come from?

Uncle Roy says he gets his in the shower, so he brings whiteboard pens into the bathroom to write on the tiles. Later, he washes off his notes. His best shower idea was deciding to save up and take six months off to learn yoga in Thailand. When he came home he was ready to work even harder for his other goals.

Here's what I figured out: once an idea sticks, even if it doesn't seem that interesting at first, it won't fizzle. It *incubates*.

The courtyard at camp has lots of shade trees that act as umbrellas, and our group has claimed one. Other groups film scenes or rehearse lines or play with equipment out in the bright sun. For the rest of camp we have flexible mornings to work on our movies however we want, even going off campus to shoot if our parents give permission. Abby's planning everything so we won't waste any time. Trey and I watch her pace and talk to herself like she's a real pro.

"Okay. We have a title: *B Is for Bakunawa*. And thanks to Kaia, we have a screenplay," Abby says. Last night I got so excited that I wrote it in thirty minutes. Trey claps and Abby shoots him her please-don't-interrupt-me glare. "We also decided on two main shooting locations—the beach and the camp cafeteria—but we'll need to do some location scouting for the beach scenes. Who's with me?"

I grab Trey's arm and stretch it high. We end up arm wrestling.

"Team B, how are we going to compete if we don't take this seriously?" She pounds her fist into her hand. "Time! Is! Money!"

"Location scouting—check!" I say.

"Dave! Get over here!" Abby shrieks across the courtyard, and Dave Conway glances up and scuttles over. Dave goes to our middle school too, and Abby's the only kid he seems to kind of listen to.

We've cast a few other Art Attackers in the supporting roles. Dave gets to play Siyokoy the merman (he's the only one who Abby made audition). Jalissa Jones will play the Sirena, and Jackson Cho is Tiyanak, the Philippine flesh-eating baby.

"Dave, we need to go over your part," Abby says. Most of our movie has no dialogue, but he gets one really fabulous line plus a tight shot on his face where Abby will zoom all the way in so you can see every detail in high definition, even his nose hairs.

"Bring it," he says.

"Watch and learn." Abby steps onto a patio table and readies herself. She peers off into the distance and shouts: "Bakunawaaaaa!"

A few kids clap.

"All right, let's see what you can do," she says to Dave.

He hops up onto the table next to Abby and lowers his head. He jerks it up, gives an intense, frightened stare, drops to his knees, lifts his fists high, and yells at the top of his lungs like he's in pain:

"Bakuuuuuunaaaaaaaawaaaaaaaaaaaaa!"

This time the whole courtyard applauds. Dave and Abby join hands and bow.

They jump down and Abby says, "Meh. Let's try it again… but with more feeling this time."

She hands him the script and I whisper in Abby's ear: "You guys would make a cute couple."

"Eww!" she says. I know she's pretending a little, because she's told me before that she might like Dave—as in like-like. Of all our friends she's the first to have crushes. The thought of like-liking someone still seems weird to me.

"What?" Dave says, and I give Abby a little smirk.

Time to focus on one thing: Trey's monstrous transformation.

We sit across from each other at a patio table, I open my makeup bag, and I pull out the silvery colors Lainey gave me before she left. I keep waiting for Lainey to call so I can tell her about our project. She'd love everything about it.

Trey closes his eyes and I get to work, brushing, painting, and sponging. Kids gather, just like when tourists stop to watch artists on the boardwalk. I hope I don't flub.

My group and I decided that we don't want the bakunawa's makeup to seem too bold, but more subtle and symbolic, like our movie. Trey has silver and charcoal scales along his temples and cheeks, and the fairest dusting of shimmer. Later I'll mold some prosthetic gills to glue onto his face and neck. Abby thinks it's artsy-fartsier this way—and that artsy-fartsy wins. That's good enough for me.

I bristle a layer of paint onto Trey's cheeks and try to blend it in.

Done.

"Can I open my eyes now?" he asks.

"Yup."

Trey peeps from me to the people watching and gives a growl. Some kids snicker.

"What's he supposed to be again? A weirdo lizard?" someone asks.

"No, a mischievous sea serpent," I say, and Trey flashes a different creepy expression.

"He looks kind of . . . constipated?" one girl says with a giggle.

Trey grabs the mirror to see for himself. "Hmmm... I'm not really getting 'scary monster' vibes yet." He mouths *Sorry, Kaia*.

I scan the courtyard and every kid looks so intense at work. We're definitely not the only group in it to win it. We'll have to step up our game.

"Let's wipe it all off and try it again," I say.

Finally, I create a look for our main character that I think captures a mysterious mood. I snap a Polaroid and show it to Trey. A few kids peer over my shoulder and the steely-eyed girl says, "Nice-looking frog."

Some of the kids laugh, but I try to ignore them. I'll get this right. I'm counting on it.

• • •

After camp, on my walk home, I wish I could tell Lainey all about my day. I text her pictures of my makeup job from earlier and wait for some hearts and exclamation points back... but nothing. She called the other day and talked to my parents, but I missed her.

I walk into the house and Tatang's in the family room on the couch, sipping his daily smoothie of mainly veggies. I pour myself a glass and join him.

"I see you edited your to-do list in the kitchen," he says.

I'm glad he noticed. "It's *our* list now, so we can fit in every single fun thing we can think of before... well... before you leave."

Tatang gives me his *I really want this drilled into your head* look that I imagine he probably used a lot on his students.

"Let's get this straight, anak. I am not saying goodbye and I am not leaving forever." He reaches over and raps his knuckles on the coffee table. "This is the next phase in my life, and yours too, huh? Besides, soon you'll be a teenager, and if you're anything like your mom and Elena were, you won't want to hang out with me much longer." He cracks a grin and I feel better.

"Tatang, what does 'learn to fly' mean on your list?" I ask.

"It's a surprise... for now."

Fair enough. It wouldn't be summertime without Tatang's surprises.

"Can I tell you what Abby, Trey, and I decided on for Beach Season?" He nods. I reveal the whole plan, and hearing it out loud sounds so good. It makes me sure of one thing: we're going to snag one of those winning spots.

"Sounds radical!" Tatang says. He wants all of the old eighties slang to come back, which makes Uncle Roy cringe.

"I'm about to work on Trey's costume. Want to help?"

"I thought you'd never ask!"

In the backyard we lay old clothes on the lawn—jeans, a plain white T-shirt, a fake white leather motorcycle jacket

Dad wore on Halloween once as Filipino Elvis—and jazz them up with light sprays of silver and scales that we paint on free-hand.

"Can I show you my screenplay? It's only a few pages."

"Yes, please."

I watch Tatang's eyes scan every line. On the last page he pauses a long time.

Does he think it's too silly to stand out for the festival's judges?

"Do you...do you like it?" I finally ask.

"I do, very much, but would it be all right if I made a few small suggestions?"

I knew it. He hates it. Except that Tatang doesn't criticize. He tells me that some bakunawas have whiskers, gills, and wings, and that depending on the region, some look more like dragons than slithering serpents, or even like monstrous birds. The gears in my head crank and turn and I come up with little changes to make. Tatang's a huge help, and inside I'm dancing. I wish we could start filming this very second.

"We're going to give you a proper screen credit, Tatang."

"Assistant to the head of makeup and costumes?"

"Nope. Executive producer!"

"Great! Now I can cross 'Become big-shot Hollywood guy' off my list." He rubs his hands together. "What's next?"

I pull some tools and jugs of powder from my desk in The Cave. Now comes the messy but fun part.

I show Tatang how to mix my secret concoction of nontoxic gelatin, although not-so-secret, I guess, since I found the recipe online. He helps me pour it into a silicone fish-scale mold. After the mold dries, we pop the scales out and lay them on a Styrofoam dummy head to figure out how to glue them to Trey's face and neck. I'll paint and blend them into his makeup.

Dad had the right idea. Jumping in feels great, and so does my alone time with Tatang—it's kind of nice not having a perfect big sister around to share him with. Now it's my turn for something between only us. It'll make my team's win even sweeter.

"Thanks for helping so much, Tatang."

"That's my job. Always has been."

I'm trying hard to feel happy for him, like Mom said, but it's tough. When he leaves, who's going to cheer everyone on?

Hmm... I wonder if winning a spot in the festival would make him see how much I need him here? Seeing us win could make him realize he'd miss out on every big moment in my life.

That's it!

I can't let him down now.

• • •

Over dinner Dad asks, "How's the movie going?"

I pull out my phone to show pictures of Trey's practice transformation, but then I remember Mom's rule: *No screens at the table.* I give her puppy-dog eyes. "Please?"

She nods and I hold up the phone.

"Scary monster!" Toby says. Now I know I'm on the right track.

"Wow, honey, Trey looks fabulous!" Mom says.

"Yeah, I love all the colors," says Dad. "Your bakunawa has a lot of depth and nuance." That's fancy for "pretty good."

Tatang's face lights up and he starts asking questions: When will you begin filming? What will the other characters look like? What props will you use?

"I can't spoil the ending, Tatang! But want to hear about the other characters?" They all give me their full attention.

My head buzzes, and I'm fast talking to get everything out. Maybe people who get good at things always feel this way, like they're accomplishing something that matters.

Trey and Abby don't have any siblings, so they get their parents' time twenty-four seven without any competition. I used to think that sounded boring, but not anymore.

Mom's phone rings from the other room.

"I'll let it go to voice mail," she says. We keep looking at my pictures, but the phone rings again. Mom excuses herself from the table.

"We still have to do some location scouting," I say, and I explain how and where.

"I've always wondered how that works," Tatang says.

"Want to come?" I ask.

Mom runs back into the room with her phone. "It's Lainey!"

she shouts, and there's my sister's face, grinning. All eyes turn her way.

"Lay-Lay! Lay-Lay!" Toby shouts.

"We've been waiting for your call!" Dad says.

"We miss you so much, anak!" Tatang says.

Dad asks her how it's going and it sets off Lainey's happy rambling: how packed with cars Manila is, her surprise and sadness traveling through shantytowns, the green of the countryside, and the roosters that crow her awake in the early mornings. Everything's exactly how Tatang has described it. "I'm having the best time!"

Everyone huddles around the phone. I've waited and waited for her to call—so why don't I feel more excited?

Finally Mom points the screen in my direction.

"Kai-Kai, I wish you were here!" Lainey hollers, but we barely talk because my family can't stop asking questions about all her adventures.

12

It's a bright, clear day, the kind where the clouds seem so white because the sky's so blue. Mom, Tatang, and I make our way across the UCLA campus. UCLA stands for the University of California, Los Angeles, and it's not far from our house. Their mascot is the Bruin, so on game days someone in a fuzzy bear costume runs around giving noogies.

Students walk in every direction. I try to figure out their majors: girls going into a building carrying tall stacks of books are engineers, a guy with a camera interviewing a girl in a suit are broadcast journalists, and two guys playing Frisbee barefoot in the courtyard are undeclared.

Since Mom's a professor in Asian American studies, I know a lot of things about my culture and its history, like how Filipinos were the first Asian group to land in the United States, or that the yo-yo was invented by a Filipino man named Pedro Flores and *yo-yo* means "come back, come back" in Tagalog— and tons of other facts that Uncle Roy tells me to tuck away in my Pinoy Pride Drawer. *Pinoy* and *Pinay* mean someone who's

Filipino, and my uncle and I want to cheer whenever we hear of someone from our culture doing extraordinary things. Tatang says it's good to know where you came from, not only in the here and now but before you ever became a dot on this planet.

I spot the lecture hall where Mom teaches and sprint to the entrance. She and Tatang catch up and we head for the elevator, but Tatang says, "Stairs, please. I need to exercise these creaky legs."

Today he's Mom's secret weapon.

Tatang's wearing his best cargo shorts, orange sneakers, and a black short-sleeved button-down covered in unicorns and stacks of books. We walk down a glossy corridor into the lecture hall, which has tiered seating, whiteboards, and a wood lectern. Mom takes her place at the lectern and I sit in the back like a real college student.

Tatang sits in the front row as people file in. He hasn't brought any note cards or slides. He told me he's winging it.

Not everyone in class is Filipino or Asian. It's like my school, with all types of bodies and faces and skin colors, people with all different stories to tell. It'd be so boring if everyone around me looked the same.

"Take your seats, please," Mom says.

Tatang scans his audience and shouts, "There are open chairs in front, folks! Don't be shy! My dentures don't bite!"

A few students chuckle.

Mom says, "All right, class. Any questions about your reading on the 1965 Immigration and Naturalization Act?"

Students listen to Mom, respond, and take notes, except for one guy who's already fallen asleep. Tatang has a great big smile as he watches Mom—the same expression he had during Lainey's graduation speech.

"We'll discuss this in more detail next class," Mom says, "but for now, let's shift gears. Today we have a very special guest speaker. You may have heard me mention him before because not only is he a decorated war hero and an immigrant who has lived and achieved the American dream but, full disclosure, he's my grandfather. I'd like to introduce you to ninety-year-old Mr. Celestino Agas." Tatang straightens and Mom says, "Take it away, Mr. Agas."

They trade places up front and he opens with a joke—one I helped him think up.

"How do you fight a lumpia?" He looks around the room but no one answers. Then he says, "You *pancit*! Get it? You *punch* it? Anybody here eat lumpia and pancit? Filipino egg rolls and noodles?" A few students groan good-naturedly. At least it got them to pay attention. "Nice to see some of you have a sense of humor. That's one of the traits I value most because I've needed it to get through many things in my long life."

Tatang's face turns serious. He begins sharing stories from his days as a young soldier in World War II. Some of these memories he's told me, but there's a lot I'm hearing for the first time. The students listen as he leaves the lectern and walks the room.

"War is hard. I was part of a catastrophic event called

the Bataan Death March. This was when seventy-five thousand captured allied soldiers—Filipinos and Americans—were forced to march from sunrise to sunset, nearly sixty-five miles across the Bataan Peninsula along Manila Bay in April of 1942. We were not given any food or water. We suffered from heat stroke and starvation. We were physically beaten along the way. Many of my friends died, some of them left to rot when we could not carry them. It could easily have been me, and there has not been a single day since that I've taken my life for granted. It's why I try to stroll each evening and watch the sun set. It's my personal marker of what I've lived through and what I still have to achieve."

Wow. I never knew that. I think of the times I got annoyed when Tatang made me take end-of-the-day walks with him when I didn't want to. No wonder sundown is when he's quietest.

Soft crying comes from a student next to me as Tatang keeps going.

"At the end of the march we were crammed into trains and brought to an internment camp. Somehow I had survived to that point, but the camp was torture, too—so many soldiers dying from disease and malnutrition, some beheaded."

Students gasp. "The Philippines was a former colony of the United States, so those of us who fought were nationals; we should have received the same benefits as all American soldiers, including citizenship. But a law was passed that stripped us of these rights. We were left unrecognized, our role erased, and we're still fighting for that recognition to this day. Sadly, it's too late for some. There are not many of us survivors left."

Every time I hear Tatang speak of his war days I can imagine him so clearly on that horrible march. I rub at little goose bumps on my arms.

The time flies as Tatang shares his memories, just like when he tells Lainey and me stories and we ask for another and another, even after Dad says, "Lights out, girls."

When the class ends, Tatang is silent and stares out at the crowd, looking a little sad.

The class applauds and Mom takes her place at the lectern. "Questions?"

No one says anything. A student's phone vibrates but the owner doesn't answer. The girl next to me sniffles and even the guy who fell asleep sits up alert.

"Not a single comment? Am I that boring?" Tatang says.

Half the arms in class shoot up. He points to one.

"How did you feel when you were marching?"

"I wanted to give up, but I thought of my family."

"What's been the hardest moment in your life?"

"Figuring out who I am."

"Yeah, sounds familiar," the student says, and everyone laughs. *Figuring out who I am* is something I've heard Lainey talk about with my parents.

Tatang says, "Keep asking questions. Ask questions of your

family and of older generations to learn not only about them, but about yourself. Share their histories."

Another arm goes up. "What's your greatest achievement?" the student asks.

Tatang points in two directions—to me and to Mom. Heads whip toward me and I stare at the floor.

More hands are raised. More answers, and each is a powerful little story. Tatang's soaking this up and I'm glad. Everyone should know about his life.

When the period ends, a bunch of students stop to thank Tatang or to shake his hand. His eyes light up, and so do mine.

• • •

"How did class go?" Dad asks that night. He, Mom, and I sit on the couch, Toby and Tatang already in bed. Talking with my parents before bedtime feels nice. Hanging out. Some kids at school get embarrassed by their parents; when they go to the mall their moms drop them off at the corner instead of walking in with them the way my mom does.

"Tatang was awesome," I say. "I even heard new war stories. I wonder why he hasn't told me some of those before?"

"Maybe it's hard for him to relive the memories," Dad says.

"Or maybe . . . maybe you've never really asked," Mom teases.

"Hey! What's that supposed to mean?" I say.

"Want to know the reason I became a teacher?" Mom says.

"Because you were always teacher's pet?"

She laughs. "When I was a kid Tatang would try to tell me what it was like when he and Nanang came to California—but I was never curious. Then in high school I did a report on American immigration, so I interviewed him. I had never seen my grandfather as a person with a full life that happened before I existed. It made me appreciate what my family had been through for me. The sad part was when I did my research, I didn't find much in history books about Filipinos, even though we've had a big role in American history. That's when I decided I wanted to help people understand how important our stories are."

"Mom, that's so cool."

"I wish I'd taken time to learn more about my history while my grandparents were alive," Dad says. "A lot of kids never get to know their great-grandparents. You're lucky, Kaia."

That bad thought sneaks back into my head: one day I won't have Tatang in my life at all.

"What happens when . . . ," I start, but I have a hard time saying what I'm thinking.

"What is it?" Mom says. "It's okay, you can ask."

"What happens . . . when Tatang passes away?"

My parents look at each other.

"We'll get to that road when we have to, but now's not that time," Mom says.

I can hear Tatang in my head:

Kaia, where are your feet?

I'm here with my parents, in our home, watching them watching me.

"Mom and Dad... are you... are you upset I don't want to be a doctor?"

"You're asking a fellow artist?" Dad chuckles. "Where's this coming from, kiddo?"

"During his lecture Tatang talked about figuring out who you are. What does that even mean?"

"I think he meant what makes us unique. And according to Tatang, each of us has at least ninety years to figure that out." Mom smiles at me.

"Everything Lainey does always seems so extra special, like deciding she's premed. Must feel pretty great to figure it out, huh?"

Dad pulls me into a squeeze. "Did I ever tell you that your lolo and lola didn't want me to go to art school? They wanted me to be a doctor or a nurse or an accountant—all the things that didn't feel like me."

"How did you know what *did*?" I ask.

"It was your grandparents' tales about growing up in the Philippines that got my imagination going—especially ones about magical creatures. I couldn't stop drawing. I like to think you get some of that from me."

"I do!" I say.

"Art is in your blood, Kaia," Mom says. "And you know, immigrants like your tatang—they're artists, too. They create a life from nothing but a dream."

My parents catch each other's eyes and smile.

"Your movie is helping Tatang's stories live on, Kaia," Dad says.

Hearing this fills me up.

• • •

It's late and our house is quiet. I've been keeping Tatang's journal under my pillow.

I pull it out.

A few more photographs bookmark some of the pages. I shake them free and they fall to my lap, faded colored squares framing Nanang and Tatang, young and happy. They're standing in front of their first American apartment next to their first car, arms around each other's waists. Nanang wears cat-eye glasses and a groovy dress, and Tatang's got a buzz cut and is wearing skinny pants.

Tatang saved up months of his janitor's salary to buy that car. They drove it everywhere—dropping Nanang off at her nursing job so she wouldn't have to take the long bus ride, adventures with their kids, seeing things he never imagined he would: the desert, the snow, Yosemite, and the Grand Canyon.

Tatang's face hasn't changed much since these pictures were taken. When we were younger he had that same determined look, only without wrinkles. If I had a time machine I could spot him in any year of his life.

I scan more pages and land on my name.

Kaia will not want me to go, I know this much is true. However, I will tell them my heart has made its decision, and I will help them through this. For my greatest desire at this moment in my long life is to return to my home country and know where my feet are. The heart can have more than one home.

After what my parents said, I'm curious about the Tatang before me.

I flip open my laptop and search for articles about Filipinos in World War II and the Bataan Death March. What I find is devastating and I can see why Tatang hasn't shared much about that piece of himself.

I scroll through headlines and one stands out: *Filipino World War II Veterans Receive Congressional Gold Medal of Honor After 75 Long Years.* I click on it. The article describes how Filipinos are finally getting recognized, seven decades after the veterans' rights were taken away. It's what Tatang talked about with Mom's students.

It looks like . . . maybe he can get his own medal awarded to him? How cool would that be? I wonder if Mom already knows about this.

I read more articles. There are steps and paperwork and I'm not so sure I understand all of it, but I have a shiny new idea.

13

The next morning Mom's in the kitchen making breakfast, rice and longuinisa—Filipino sausage. Dad likes to say how the only constant thing in our ever-changing lives is the rice cooker. We pretty much eat rice with every meal. The first time I spent the night at Abby's I was surprised when they didn't offer any at breakfast. She thought that sounded weird, but she's stayed at my house so many times that Abby eats rice for breakfast at her house now too.

The room smells savory. "Morning, sweetie," Mom says.

"Good morning." I sit at the island and watch Mom crack open some eggs that sizzle when they hit the pan. "Mom, are you teaching any more classes this week?"

"Sure am. Why?"

"Could I go with you again?"

She looks at me. "Again? Really?"

"Yeah. I thought that was super interesting with Tatang.

I've never heard you do a whole lecture before. I promise I won't fall asleep like that one guy."

"It's a date."

• • •

After breakfast, Tatang and I meander down streets of palm trees, houses, apartments, and condos, on our way to meet Trey and Abby at the pier. Time to find the perfect place to shoot.

"Look!" I say, spotting a For Sale sign with Uncle Roy's picture on it. I run to it and jump with my arms raised. Tatang takes a photo and it looks like I'm taking off to soar. He texts it to my uncle and right away Uncle Roy replies with three thumbs up and a blowing kisses emoji.

We end at the shopping area along the Promenade, where Trey and Abby dash up to us. Tatang cups their faces and says things like, "Abby, when did you get braces?" and "Trey, you're as tall as I am now!"

"Ready to help us with some location scouting?" Abby asks. She hooks her arm into Tatang's and talks his ear off about B Is for Bakunawa.

We make our way to the pier, stopping at a bench with an ocean view. Tatang sits and people-watches as Abby peers around and takes pictures.

"It might be too noisy to film here," she says.

A good location scout knows that the sun rises in the east and sets in the west. Sometimes the right location means having the right feeling, a mood. So far what we've found isn't quite right. We keep looking for the perfect place to film our opening scene, where the bakunawa emerges from the sea and wanders around the beach before going off to his first day of baking school.

Trey points to an empty area without a lot of vendors. "How about over there?"

Abby points her camera lens and the shutter clicks. Tatang tags behind, stopping at the different stands to try on sunglasses and octopus hats where the tentacles dangle over his face. After a while he looks at his watch.

"Hey, kids, how about a preproduction break?" he says.

"Definitely," Trey says. I'm actually surprised Trey didn't ask to take five sooner—when he's not acting he's more of the loungey type. In his third grade All About Me presentation he told our class his favorite hobby was "couch potato-ing."

"Let's do it. Although I'm thinking of something more like an experience than a break." Tatang points up. We follow his gaze all the way to Pier Pressure, a roller coaster.

Trey starts laughing. "Tatang, you're sneaky."

I can't help but think that Mom would hate this. High rickety rides make her nervous—like me.

"You really want to go on that?" I try to sound like it's no big deal.

Tatang nods. "It's on my list!"

"But it's so . . . high. Plus, I don't think Mom would like this."

"It'll be okay, anak. I'll go buy the tickets." Tatang scurries off to a ticket window, where he chats with the guy behind the register, a long line of antsy people waiting.

"You have the coolest great-grandpa ever," Trey says. I can't argue with that.

Soon Tatang hands each of us a paper stub. "Ready?"

• • •

Some kids love roller coasters. They live for the speed, for the thrill of the drop. A lot of kids from school go to Disneyland during break and wait for hours in long lines, then do it all over again—and again and again. The closer we get to the front of the line, the more I know I'm not one of those people. This roller coaster looks too high and loopy, but I can't not ride it now, not when my best friends *and* a man who's ninety act like it's nothing.

We inch our way up in line. Almost our turn.

I start to feel nauseous.

"Are you positive you want to do this?" I ask, but they don't even hear me. They're watching the ride overhead and listening to passengers shrieking.

"That looks *soooo* scary," Abby says, but with a gigantic grin.

I shove my hands into my pockets and squeeze them tight.

We reach the front and the cars glide along the track toward us, slowing to a stop. People get off and the attendant opens a small gate to let us through.

"Here we go, kids!" Tatang says, and I take a huge breath.

Each car holds four people and Trey and Abby sit behind us. We're in the very front car.

"Perfect seats, Tatang. We'll feel every twist and turn!" Abby shouts.

Yeah. Perfect.

We pull a thick black bar down across our laps and I push it up a few times to make sure it's locked tight and we won't slip out.

Please please please don't throw up.

Tatang looks behind us. "Feeling good, Abigail and Trey?"

They yell at the top of their lungs: "Wooooooo!"

Slowly the cars climb toward the sky, ratcheting up along the rickety tracks. I clamp my eyes shut.

"It's okay, Kaia, you can look!" Tatang says. "Let's take in the scenery!"

I open one eye—and eventually both.

Is this thing safe?

We soar higher and higher until I see the ocean to one side and mountains to the other. It's the prettiest view. Everything looks miniature, and somehow that makes things all right.

Then, a drop and a scream—mine!

• • •

I'm out of breath from yelling.

My stomach dropped a billion times and my nerves are still rattling around, but the ride only lasted a few minutes, and once I gave in it was pure fun. Now I get it: sometimes it's best to try.

"That. Was. Epic!" Trey shouts. He and Tatang high-five.

"Oh my, I have not done anything like that in *years*. Thank you, children, for indulging me."

Tatang's phone buzzes and Mom's picture pops up. He touches the screen and laughs into it. In Ilocano he says, "I just took the kids on Pier Pressure!"—followed by him saying in English, "We are fine. Every limb and leg accounted for, I promise."

Soon, Trey's mom, Vanessa, picks Abby and Trey up at a curb and offers to drive me and Tatang too, but we say no thank you. Everyone waves as they drive off.

"How do you do it, Tatang?" I ask as we walk home.

"Do what?"

"Weren't you scared to go on that crazy ride?"

"Why, certainly. You never know how safe those things are!"

The first thing we see when we get home is Mom's scowl. She shakes her head. "Tatang, a man your age should not be doing thrill rides."

"Please, my dear, tell me exactly what should a man my age be doing? I've had too much heartbreak in my life to not revel in the good stuff, am I right?"

When Tatang speaks of heartbreak, I think he means Nanang Cora. She had a type of cancer doctors couldn't fix, and after she died, the family story is that Tatang got very sad in a way no one could fix either. I've never seen that side of him. Whenever he speaks of Nanang his face shows so many different emotions. "It's because we feel with our hearts, not with our brains," he's told me.

"Come here, take a look," Tatang says to Mom. He pulls out a photo strip we all took in a booth after the ride. We're squished together in different poses: scared, surprised, goofy, giddy. "This was *after* the roller coaster. I happen to know how very nervous Kaia was at first—but see?"

"You knew I felt nervous?" I ask, and he nods.

"Our little girl isn't so little anymore, is she?" he says to Mom. The corners of his mouth turn up. "You did it, anak! You conquered your fear."

His look makes me feel as if I'm the most important person in the world to him.

14

Filming. Day one. Venice Beach.

Big day!

Balmy gray fills the sky. Locals call this June Gloom. It's overcast, perfect to film in because the camera won't pick up harsh shadows. Luckily this dull sky doesn't match our mood. Abby, Trey, and I sport huge grins: we're about to shoot our first scene.

Trey's in full makeup and costume, thanks to Tatang's help the other day. He looks equal parts beautiful and evil. Yes! I did pretty awesome for my first monster movie.

We hop into Abby's mom's electric car, which is covered in political bumper stickers, and Sam drives us to a beachside parking lot. Trey, Abby, and I get out and pull equipment from the trunk.

"I'll be going for my run while you kids do your thing. You've got your phones in case you need to call, right?" Sam says to Abby.

"Yes! Thanks!" we say before shuffling down the sand to

find our lucky spot. My pockets jingle full of coins—I grabbed some this morning. Normally we do this on New Year's; it's a Filipino tradition for wealth and good luck. But I don't see why it wouldn't work now.

We spread out a blanket and throw our stuff on top. Abby pulls out the camera.

At camp we blocked and rehearsed everything so today will be smooth and easy. Eliza likes to remind our class that anything can happen during production, but I think we're safe. Abby created our shot list and has kept us super organized. At school she has the tidiest locker of anyone, with her mirror, carpet square, and pictures arranged and tacked up with heart magnets like it's a mini-gallery. We're in good hands.

Today's scene: the bakunawa will emerge from the ocean before going to The Summer Baking Institute of Magical Sweets.

"Let's do it!" I say.

Abby brings Trey to a spot a few feet out from the water, with peaceful waves in the background. She marks the sand with her foot.

"I want you to go from here all the way to that palm tree," she points.

The clouds part and out of nowhere, sunshine slices through. It's soft and dreamy, a kind of magic before Bakunawa tricks them all. Now we're ready.

I show Trey the storyboards I roughed out:

SCENE #: 1	SHOT #: 2	SHOT SIZE:

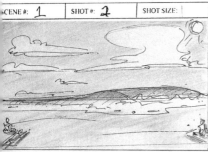

Clouds, Sunshine, waves

SCENE #: 1	SHOT #: 3	SHOT SIZE: MS

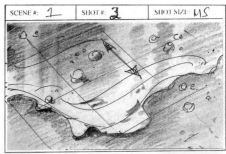

White foam bubbles
onto shore.

SCENE #: 1	SHOT #: 3	SHOT SIZE: CU

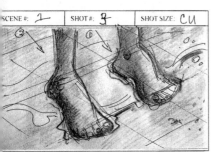

One foot steps onto sand,
then another.

SCENE #: 1	SHOT #: 4	SHOT SIZE: MS

Pan up to see Bakunawa
fresh from the sea.

SCENE #: 1	SHOT #: 5	SHOT SIZE: CU

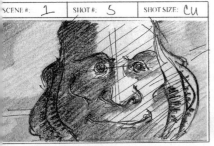

Mischievous glint in his
beady little eyes.

SCENE #: 1	SHOT #: 6	SHOT SIZE:

Off he goes...

"Okay, Bakunawa, you've just emerged from the depths of the sea and you're walking down the beach. The audience has no clue who you are...yet. Right now your job is to keep our viewers guessing," Abby says.

"I can do that," Trey says.

He won't actually emerge from the ocean, so I pull out a spray bottle of water and lightly mist his hair to make it look like he has. I put my hand to his forehead like a visor so his makeup won't slide off.

I grab the slate board and stand in front of the camera. Trey waits for his signal.

"Scene one, take one!" I say into the lens before stepping out of the way.

Abby shouts, "Aaaaaaand...action!"

Trey centers himself and stares down the grainy landscape.

EXT. VENICE BEACH—MORNING

Clouds. Sunshine. Ocean waves lapping in.

White foam bubbles onto the shore peacefully before retreating. A typical Southern California day.

Until . . .

One shiny, silver bare foot steps onto the sand.
Then another.

We pan up to see BAKUNAWA, fresh from the sea.

Bakunawa is part man and part aquatic creature.

He has a muscular build, silvery, shiny scales, and a mischievous glint in his beady little eyes.

Bakunawa's never been on land before. He peers around.

He seems innocent enough, cheerfully taking everything in as he walks down the shore.

Bakunawa takes one step forward, and another, getting farther and farther from the ocean.

Trey moves from his mark and turns his head every which way, exactly how Abby directed, when something white plops onto his face.

He touches it, stares at his hand, and yelps in horror.

"Cut!" Abby shouts. "What happened?"

"Ewwwwwwww!" he shouts. "Bird turd!"

I hold my stomach from laughing so hard. Abby's not amused.

"Umm... take two?" I say.

Abby gives us a five-minute break for me to fix Trey's makeup. I wipe the gross slime off his cheek as he tries to stop himself from dry heaving.

"Can we call it a day now?" he says, but our director shakes her head.

"Are you kidding? We can't let a little thing like poop get in the way of making the best movie of all time, can we?" Trey and I nod—we don't have any other choice. "Good," Abby says. "Let's move, move, move!"

We try to get more shots of Trey sauntering down the beach.

During one take, Abby stands along the edge of the bike path for a wide shot, but as soon as she yells "Action!" the camera lens gets blocked by a clump of bicyclers pedaling by.

"Cut!"

During another take, a gust of wind sweeps sand into the camera and into Trey's mouth and eyes. He rubs at his face and spits it out.

"Cut!"

"I can't do this anymore!" Trey yells.

"One more time, Bakunawa—I believe in you!" Abby yells back.

I touch up Trey's scales. He tries the scene again while Abby points to where he needs to go. As we start to film, a guy in a uniform riding a Segway rolls up to us. He seems... kind of official?

"Beachside security. Do you have a permit to be filming here?" he asks.

"This is for camp, it's nothing professional," Abby says.

"Then move it along, move it along. Darn kids!" he barks out, before backing up and rolling away in the other direction.

"Is he serious?" Trey says.

"It's okay. Maybe we can find a different beach to shoot at," I say, trying to stay positive like Abby, but she shakes her head.

"I'm not feeling it anymore. Trey's right. We should call it quits," Abby says.

My brain thinks we need to keep plugging on, but truthfully, I'm done too.

We pack up and find a bench to wait for Abby's mom. A few minutes later Sam spots us.

"How'd it go, Team B?"

"Horrible," Trey explains. "It's like we're cursed."

I touch my pocket, remembering the coins. If I told Mom we needed good luck today, she probably would have made me do a few extra superstitions.

"Oh, I'm sure it's not as bad as you think," Sam says.

I'm ready for an excellent Abby Pep Talk, but her face droops. Abby slings the camera bag onto her shoulder as she walks to the car and says, "Back to the drawing board, people."

• • •

At home I find Uncle Roy and Tatang posing in matching headstands, their heads planted onto the cream-colored carpet, forearms firmly on the ground and feet up against the wall. Music plays—something with waterfalls and chirping birds. I Filipino-squat near them and Tatang grins. They gently lower themselves down and rest before sitting up. I reach for two bottles of water to hand them.

"I've still got it, huh, Roy-Roy?" Tatang says.

"Not bad for an old dude," Uncle Roy says. "How'd filming go, Kaia Papaya?"

Tatang peers my way and his eyes brighten. If I want him

to brag about me to everyone at Ocean Gardens, I can't let on that we bombed.

"It went... okay." I try to smile and seem natural but I don't meet his eyes.

He looks pleased. "I'm about to run some errands. Care to join me?"

I nod. I could use a good distraction.

• • •

We drive to a nearby strip mall but when we pull in, every single spot's taken. Usually we'd circle until something opens up—or until Dad gets mad and says with a hmph, "Fine, I'll pay for overpriced valet!" and Mom gets annoyed he didn't do that to begin with.

Tatang drives slowly down a lane while I scan for an empty space.

"Come on, parking karma!" I say, hoping for some good luck. Behind us a car beeps. A long loud blare.

We keep rolling at a snail's pace when that same car pulls up close behind. It honks again, then swings around to our side.

My window's wide open—so is the driver's—and he's shouting at us even though we didn't do anything wrong. "You're holding up the line, old man!"

Tatang sees an open spot a few spaces up. I think the guy sees it too and he drives forward, but Tatang races and beats him. We take the space.

"What an idiot driver," Tatang says. He surprises me—Tatang never uses insults or strong words, and always gets mad at me when I do.

"Yeah, what an idiot," I say.

Tatang turns the engine off. He takes a few steadying breaths, pauses, and looks me straight in the eye.

"Kaia, that's not at all appropriate—and the same goes for what I just said. I'm very sorry, anak. My reaction was unacceptable. It was rude and uncalled for."

"But he was the rude one."

Tatang's face isn't scrunched up anymore. His anger has drained.

"We don't know that individual and I don't take what he said personally. What I do know is that how people treat others is a direct reflection of themselves."

I apologize too and we take care of his errands. Once we're done, Tatang points to a coffee shop. "Mind if we pop in? I could use some caffeine."

Tatang orders his very fancy drink and I spot the rude driver standing behind us, reading the menu.

"Here ya go." The girl behind the counter slides the cup to Tatang.

"May I ask your name?" Tatang says with a smile.

She returns it. "Roslyn."

Quietly he responds, "Roslyn, I'd also like to pay for the gentleman's order behind me, please."

"Excuse me?"

"You'll make my day, Roslyn, if you help us out."

He hands her a bill and we don't wait for the change. As we leave Tatang looks that man in the eyes and says, "Have a good day."

We head to our car, but the guy pops up *again*. I grab Tatang's hand. "Let's go," I say, but it's too late. The man approaches us, though his grimace has disappeared.

"Sir, I, ummm...," the man says. "I'm, uhhh... Look. Sorry about earlier. I was having the worst day, but that's no excuse. Thank you for the coffee. I appreciate it."

Tatang extends his hand and they shake.

How does my great-grandpa do that—bring out every kindness in people?

As we walk off, I ask, "Why were you so nice to that guy when he wasn't?"

"My dear Kaia, I always go for the more challenging choice."

15

I sit at the kitchen island with my mom while we wait for Trey and Abby to come by. Mom's writing something down and slips the paper toward me.

"What do you think of this menu for Tatang's going-away party?" She rattles off a few dishes and a schedule of eating and karaoke-ing, our family's favorite things.

"He's going to love it."

Getting ready for Beach Season has helped me take my mind off Tatang leaving—but I can't keep avoiding it.

"Do you think Tatang felt bad when he left the Philippines for California?" I ask.

She looks surprised, but thoughtful. "It's hard to leave what's familiar, Kaia. He's going back to his heart."

It reminds me of a documentary that Lainey, Dad, and I watched about sea turtles. Certain species of sea turtles spend most of their time in the ocean but will return to their birthplace to lay eggs. Even if they're thousands of miles away, they use the Earth's magnetic field as a guide back to the place they're always connected to. Home.

"Mom, how much more time before Tatang goes?"

She gets up to look at the calendar on the wall, and I join her.

"Getting closer . . . Around a month and a half now. But I'm excited for his new journey. Let's keep doing our best to help him prep." She sighs. Her words don't match how she really feels.

My fingers trace the calendar's squares, following a trail to the Beach Season deadline. We have a little more than a couple weeks.

• • •

Prop time.

We're getting ready for our next scene: the bakunawa's first day of pastry school. We'll film it in the camp cafeteria tomorrow, but today Abby and Trey have come over to rehearse in the kitchen.

We open and close cupboards. "Should I turn on some music?" I ask. "Let's pretend we're on a baking show."

If there's anything my family does well together, it's watching cooking shows. By the end of each episode I'm wishing I could reach through the screen to taste things.

Trey picks a playlist on my phone and turns up the volume. We bob our heads to a beat, plucking out boxes of cake mix, tubs of icing, bowls, mixers, and measuring cups.

In our story, Bakunawa gobbles up the other cooks' sweet sun cakes until they chase him away by banging on metal pans. This climax scene is what's going to cinch our spot in the contest.

Uncle Roy comes in—he raids our pantry whenever his gets empty. Mom hates it but she says that's what little brothers do. It makes me wonder how Toby and I will act when we're grown-ups.

"Kaia and crew!" Uncle Roy opens the fridge, takes out orange juice, and swigs straight from the bottle.

"Don't let Mom see that," I say.

He picks up a cake box and scans it. "Whatcha up to?"

"Baking props for the scene we're shooting tomorrow," Abby says, dumping cake mix into a bowl. A powdery cloud poufs up. "Is this how we do it?" she asks, coughing and waving it away. Abby and her mom don't cook much at home.

"Whoa, whoa, whoa. Hold. Up." Uncle Roy raises the box to his face to get a closer look. "Red dye number 40 . . . monocalcium phosphate . . . propylene glycol? These are chemicals used in antifreeze and fertilizer! This stuff's gonna kill you!"

"Yuck, I never knew that." Abby takes a step back from her mixing bowl.

Uncle fans himself like he might faint. "Kaia, you call yourself my niece? Shame on you! In this family from now on we bake from *scratch!*"

"Rude," I whisper to Trey, and he snorts.

"Why didn't you rug rats ask me to help?"

I shrug. "You're always busy." Uncle Roy's laptop calendar gets so full that he has to put sticky notes on his screen just so he remembers everything. We like to tease him about that.

"Puh-leeze. Am I not the only legitimate baker in this family? Okay, outta my way," he huffs, throwing the cake mix box into the recycling bin.

Uncle Roy starts doling out orders—soon the counter is covered in natural ingredients like flour, eggs, butter, sugar, and vanilla; we start measuring and pouring, sifting and beating. We taste a quick sample.

Trey licks his lips. "Mmm!" he says. I agree.

Our cakes go into the oven and the kitchen starts to smell sugary and wonderful. When Uncle Roy holds open houses, he has a trick: he bakes cookies in whatever house he's selling because the pleasant smell reminds people of their childhoods and it gives them the warm fuzzies as they tour the place.

By afternoon's end we're baking four perfect round cakes, plus some cupcakes we'll eat with our crew after we wrap filming.

As we finish cleaning up, Abby says, "Okay, let's go over the schedule."

"Again?" Trey says, but she reads down her shot list, alternating between making notes and eyeing us to make sure we're listening.

The timer dings. I open the oven to peek in.

"It smells delicious!" Trey's eyes are wide.

I turn off the oven, slip on some mitts, and carefully pull out our delectable props. "Smells like victory to me," I say.

Tatang comes in, sniffing. "This smells like a celebration!"

"We'll definitely celebrate with cake at our red carpet premiere," says Abby.

"Does this mean I'll have to stick around a while longer to watch you all get famous if you win?" Tatang winks at her.

I lean in to my great-grandpa and ask, into his ear, "Do you think we have a good chance?"

"Whatever happens, anak, I'm sure your determination will be rewarded."

I'll take that as a yes.

I know Tatang's joking about sticking around, but he won't feel that way much longer. I'll be giving him the best reason to stay.

● ● ●

I wake and the sun's already up.

Today's a huge shooting day at camp. I jump out of bed, get ready, and skip downstairs. Tatang's friend Harold beams at me from his seat on the couch.

"There she is, my favorite filmmaker!"

I take a flouncy bow. "Tatang told you about our movie?"

"He can't stop yapping about it! Everyone at the Gardens is living for his updates, Kaia. And if for some reason Celestino can't be your date to the big premiere, I know thirty or so seniors who'd be willing to step in. I have a purple velvet tuxedo, by the way."

I laugh. "Thanks. You'll get to see the film when we're finished." Harold lifts his palm for a high-five.

I wonder how Tatang will feel leaving one of his best friends—they're so close. "Harold, were you surprised when Tatang told you about his move?"

"Sometimes it may seem like Celestino does things on a whim, but his choices are always intentional." Harold pats my arm. "You still thinking about that?"

"Of course, but it doesn't matter because I thought of a way to change his mind!"

He chuckles. "Well, one day you'll travel the world too, young lady, and maybe you'll see what it's like to miss a place when one of your homes is thousands of miles away. I don't think it'll be so easy for you to sway your great-grandfather, but who knows? Maybe you'll surprise me," he says. "You joining us on our walk this morning?"

"I wish I could." I lead Harold into the kitchen and show him our cakes and cupcakes, packed neatly in pink bakery boxes from Uncle Roy. "Mom's helping me deliver these to camp so we can finish filming."

Harold grins. "Keep me posted."

16

My morning at camp started with helping other kids on their films—same with Abby and Trey—but now it's time for our own.

Filming. Day two. Camp cafeteria.

We've recruited our campmates for today's complicated scene. Everyone works together putting up lights and microphones, lining the kitchen counter with mixing bowls and big wooden spoons, and dusting flour around. Once we're done it doesn't look like a high school cafeteria anymore, but a real live baking school.

Our actors stand on set in costume and makeup, taking pictures of themselves while waiting for Abby to tell them what to do.

Today we have:

Dave Conway in the role of Siyokoy the Merman. I've given Dave the coolest look of bright aquamarine scales and little gills I molded and stuck to his neck with makeup glue.

There's Jalissa Jones, a beautiful Sirena, with glittery

bluish green and pink scales swept across her cheekbones, wave-shaped. She's wearing a green leotard from last year's school musical about healthy eating (*Peas on Earth*), when she played an asparagus (I was Avocado Number Four).

Lastly, Jackson Cho is an evil vampire disguised as a baby called Tiyanak. I've painted dark shadows around his eyes and splattered fake blood around his mouth. He'd freak me out if we ever ran into each other in an empty alleyway.

Each character is so much better than any Halloween costume. I snap photos of my creations and text them to Lainey, even though I have no idea when she'll see them.

Abby reviews the scene with our actors while Eliza checks in.

"Looks like you've got it covered, Art Attackers. Good luck." She waves as she leaves.

I read through our scene one last time.

INT. SUMMER BAKING INSTITUTE OF
MAGICAL SWEETS KITCHEN—DAY

Sunlight through a window.

A counter piled high with pots and pans.

Powdery flour . . . everywhere.

Four eager students—Bakunawa, the SIYOKOY,
the SIRENA, and the TIYANAK—are in the
kitchen, baking cakes for a class project.

They're mixing. They're tasting. They're having
a blast.

Bakunawa does his best, a big smile plastered on his face, but it quickly turns into confusion. Compared to the other talented bakers he's way out of his league.

The creatures pour their batters into pans.

One by one each pan of smooth cake batter goes into the oven.

Hands on a clock move in fast forward.

INSERT SIGN: *One Hour Later*

DING! The timer goes off.

The cakes are baked and finished now—and magically iced! They look delicious. Amazing. Mind-blowing!

Well . . . except for Bakunawa's. As soon as he sets his on the stainless steel countertop it SPLATS and FARTS. It sinks.

The other creatures glance over to Bakunawa's ugly cake and give each other amused, braggy smirks.

The CAMERA TIGHTENS on Bakunawa's face. His eyes get wide—and rascally. He licks his lips.

When the other creatures aren't looking . . .

. . . we see a pair of silver scaly hands reach up to the counter and slide the first cake away.

Bakunawa runs into a hidden corner and greedily gobbles it up, though the others don't see him.

Siyokoy, Sirena, and Tiyanak turn back to look at their perfect cakes—and notice that one is missing.

What happened?!

They hunt around, and when their backs are turned, the same pair of silver hands steals the next cake.

CUT TO Bakunawa shoving more glorious goodness into his mouth. He finishes. He lets out a huge BURP.

> BAKUNAWA
> (sheepishly)
> Excuse me.

Once again, silver hands reach up, only this time . . .

. . . all eyes go to Bakunawa.

He peers up at three angry, glaring faces.

Caught!

Siyokoy, Sirena, and Tiyanak shoot dagger looks at Bakunawa, who's about to eat the third cake.

> SIYOKOY
> (confused)
> What the?????

Siyokoy reaches for Bakunawa. Panic ensues and Bakunawa gets up, clutching the cake.

INT. SUMMER BAKING INSTITUTE OF
MAGICAL SWEETS DINING HALL—DAY

SIYOKOY
Bakuuuunaaawaaaaaa!

Bakunawa hangs on to the cake and runs through
the kitchen and into the dining hall.

Siyokoy, Sirena, and Tiyanak grab metal pots and
pans and giant metal and wood spoons from the
counter, and BANG on them as loudly as they can,
following close behind Bakunawa.

All day we shoot the baking and eating scene beat by beat,
and so far, so good. We have one part left to film: when the
creatures grab pans to chase Bakunawa away with their loud
noises.

Abby says, "Nice work, crew. Take five, everyone—you de-
serve it!"

She's right: our group's awesome and they've given this
their all. They're tired, but we've almost got this.

"Are we done yet? I'm starving," Dave asks, and the other
actors nod, except for Trey, who's already been chowing down
on cake for these scenes.

"We'll get our reward soon," I say. I can't picture a better celebration than raising our cupcakes in a cheer once we
wrap. We'll be one step closer to the red carpet.

"They're going to be the best things you've ever tasted,"
Trey says to Dave.

Abby turns to me. "Is everyone back now?"

"Looks like it."

Dave, Jalissa, and Jackson wait at their marks while Trey crouches in the corner, holding the plate of cake before we film him getting chased away.

Abby says, "Quiet on the set, please!" Silence. She shouts, "Sound!"

I hold out a long boom stand with a microphone at the end and call out, "Speed!"

"And camera!" one crew member shouts.

"Camera rolling!" shouts another.

"Mark it!" I say.

"Scene four, take one, marker!" a crew member says, clapping the black-and-white slate board, then stepping out of the shot.

"Aaaaand... action!"

Trey grips the plate. Looming over him are the faces of three very angry monsters. He springs up and sprints through the cafeteria.

Dave, Jalissa, and Jackson grab pots, pans, and spoons and bang fiercely while chasing him—until Trey trips.

What happens next feels like I'm watching it in slow-mo.

Trey falls face-first into the cake. Dave, Jalissa, and Jackson skid to a stop behind him, tripping and piling up like a train wreck.

Icing flies. Bodies tangle. Pots clink and scatter.

"Oh. My. Gosh," Abby says, and the room goes dead quiet.

Until Dave Conway starts laughing. He swipes his finger into icing smashed on the ground and licks it. "Woo-hoo! I've been waiting all day!"

"You think this is funny?" Trey says, wiping frosting from his eyes. "I can't believe I did that. I'm so sorry, Abbs... I ruined the shot!" His face crumples. "And the makeup."

Abby looks over to me in horror. "What just happened?"

Dave looks at me, mouth full of cake. "Mmm... hey, Kaia, did your uncle bake this?"

Trey takes a chunk of cake and flings it into Dave's face. Dave does the same thing back but instead it lands on Jackson, who reaches for a fistful and chucks—it lands on poor Jalissa.

"Food fight!" someone shouts.

Soon the cafeteria is all shrieks and arms and cake flinging. Abby and I charge in, trying to stop everyone.

"What are you doing?" Abby shouts, running around frantically. A gob of cake smacks onto her forehead.

If Eliza comes in she'll kill us—but as soon as Abby and I make eye contact, I can't help myself: I reach for squishy icing and hurl it at her. She shrieks just as the cafeteria doors swing open.

Eliza stands there, eyes wide, fists on her hips. Slowly she looks around the room.

We all freeze.

"I can explain—" Abby says, but Eliza holds up a hand. "You have twenty minutes to clean up. If I see even a crumb of cake *anywhere,* I'm shutting down production. *Understood?*"

We nod hard.

She gives us the teeniest secret smile and says, "Carry on," before turning and closing the door behind her.

When we can no longer hear Eliza's footsteps, we all bust up.

Of course our shot was ruined. Of course we have no more props to use. But we can't stop laughing as we clean it all up.

A few campers help me redo our characters' makeup and we convince the crew to stay late for retakes. It's more hard work, but by the end we're killing it. The fun of making something has kept us going, and I hear one crew member say to another, "Their movie's going to be so good."

I can't wipe the smile off my face, especially when I bring out the last pink box, open it, and say, "Who's ready for cupcakes?"

17

Filming. Day three. Venice Beach... again.

Trey sits at my bedroom mirror in makeup and new scales, practicing different expressions. There's a picture on the wall above him of Lainey at the beach with her surfboard, smiling our way like she approves. She'll be so surprised at how much better I've gotten at my art. She was right. Practice and trying new things have made a big difference.

"I look... awesome!" he says.

Please please please let today work out, I think.

"Let's go." We grab our stuff and meet Uncle Roy and Abby downstairs.

Uncle studies Trey's face up close. "My niece, the artiste," he says in a little rhyme, and I grin.

We hop into Uncle's car and soon pull into a spot by the Venice Pier. I wonder how it looks to strangers as we get out—three regular people and a sea monster.

"I'm making some open house flyers, so I'll be in there," Uncle says, nodding to a coffee shop. He gives us the corniest wink. "Text me when you're done or if you need anything, okay?"

Abby motors ahead, parks her stuff on a bench, and sets up the camera.

Today is reshoots, then camp this afternoon. Dad helped me call the city about permits and they said we didn't need one for a school or camp project, that sometimes they have overzealous beach security. Whew. We're all set.

Abby draws an X in the sand. "Trey, start here and I'll film you as you walk to that palm tree. You're looking around . . . you're excited about your first day of baking school. And more than anything you're ready to make your mark in this world. Got it?"

"Aye-aye, sir," Trey says.

"Good. Fingers crossed no interruptions this time," she says.

"Or bird turds," I say, and Trey pretends to gag.

I spot every little thing that could go wrong: kids chasing each other on the sand, a group of teenagers blasting music, and seagulls that might use Trey as their target. But today will be perfect because Tatang said we'll have two cakes at his party—one for his going away, and the other to celebrate our movie. He knows we're going to win.

Suddenly my hands feel clammy. I glance down at my sneakers on the sand.

We take our positions.

"Scene one, take one!" I shout, snapping the slate board.

"Aaaaand... action!" Abby says.

Trey walks from one point to the other.

What's going through Trey's head as he pretends? Most of the time I like who I am, but it's fun to imagine Opposite Me: a sports person, a popular girl on Pep Squad, a straight-A student.

I watch Trey's subtle expressions—he's acing this.

Abby peeps her head out from behind the camera and shouts, "Cut!"

People stop to watch. One young couple even claps.

"How was that?" Trey asks, and we look to our director.

"Don't forget us when you're famous," Abby says with a big smile.

"What are you guys filming?" ask the clappers.

"A story we made up," I say.

"About what?"

"About finding out what makes you special," Abby replies.

We finish and pack up.

"That was fun," Trey says.

"For how much we've bombed, we're doing pretty fabulous," I say.

"Agreed," Abby says, pulling out her calendar. "We're ahead of schedule, too."

I raise my palm for a high five. "Red carpet, here we come!"

• • •

Once we get to camp, we dash into class and grab bean bags.

Chatter and murmurs fill the classroom as Eliza yanks down a large projection screen.

Today we get a sneak peek of everyone's movies. Trey, Abby, and I chose clips from our very best footage. At first Abby didn't want to show anything at all—she wanted to keep ours a surprise—but Trey said, "Let's make them all sweat."

The lights dim. One by one each group shows a tiny bit. They're all okay, but honestly, none really stand out yet. Ours still has the most elaborate makeup and an exciting story that's never been done before.

"All right. Next up, Group Bakunawa." Abby gives me a thumbs-up. Eliza hits play on her computer.

As soon as Bakunawa appears on the screen, I scan the other kids' reactions.

"Whoa," I hear a voice say.

Someone else says, "Nice!"

Campers nod—they seem impressed.

I elbow Abby and she covers her grin with both hands, like she's about to squeal.

After the screenings it's break, and as we all herd out one kids says, "That bakunawa one was *sooooo* good."

The girl with the steely eyes taps me on the shoulder. I brace for something snarky but she says, "You're getting into Beach Season for sure."

Now I know we have something special.

18

Look up. What do you see?

Mom and I walk through campus and I can hear Tatang's voice in my head as I get a glimpse of the sky above. Sometimes seeing a vast blue sky overhead gives me that same feeling as when I dip into the cool ocean, or when I can see the sprawling city on a clear day after we've hiked to the top of a canyon. Moments that make me feel like I can do anything.

We enter the lecture hall and I sit in a back row again. This'll be Lainey soon. Tatang always says how in America people have options with or without college degrees, but for him, growing up in the Philippines, the only way out of poverty was through education. His elementary school had one classroom with all the grades together, plus a monkey outside who climbed coconut trees and distracted him and his classmates.

Tatang became a teacher because he wanted to help kids reach their goals like he did. I guess that's why he loves it so much when Lainey shows off her report cards.

People trickle in and take their seats, open up their

laptops or notebooks, and don't notice me. The guy in front of me—the same student who slept through half of Tatang's lecture—wears headphones and I can hear muffled music. I should probably warn him that Mom hates that (she always complains about how it's so rude when she's teaching), but she gives him a steady stare and that's enough for him to look embarrassed and put them away.

"Any questions on U.S. colonial and neocolonial history in the Philippines?" Mom asks, and hands go in the air.

Once the hour ends, students shut their books and pack up. I run down to the crowd in front of the room. A few students approach Mom to chat.

"I'll only be a few minutes, Kaia," she says.

That was my plan all along.

"I'll wait outside," I say as I file into the hallway with the rest of the students. I look for the friendliest faces. One girl reminds me a little bit of Lainey, with long, shiny black hair past her shoulders.

I tap her shoulder quietly.

She seems surprised, but then smiles. "Oh, you're Dr. Santos's daughter. It's Kaia, right? My name's Avery. She's talked about you in class."

"She has?"

"Yeah, she talks about you guys all the time. Especially your sister, Lainey."

Right. Oh well, at least the girl knows my name.

"Yeah, sooo... um... I was wondering if you can help me with something," I say, glancing through the open door. Mom's still chatting. "But I don't want my mom to know about it... yet. I'm trying to surprise my family."

"Ooh, this is gonna be good!" says the sleeping earphones guy, but the girl nudges him.

"Are you okay?" Avery asks.

"Don't worry, it's nothing bad. Can I tell you about it?"

"Definitely," she says, and we step outside to bright skies.

I share my idea and Avery seems eager to help. What I want to do for Tatang is something Mom may already be planning—she's so on top of these things—but I don't know for sure. I'm hoping Avery can help me find out.

"There's an application too, but it's really confusing."

"Let's look at the website," Avery says, and we read through it on her phone. She takes out some paper and we write a list of answers I need to get from Tatang for the application. The tricky part will be asking him questions without giving away my plan.

"I'll find out first if your mom knows anything about it. Then we'll both do some research, and I'll help you with the form. Does that work?" she asks.

"That would be so amazing, thank you!"

"Here's my number." She writes it down on the sheet and hands it to me.

"Please don't tell anyone yet," I say.

"My lips are sealed." She pretends to zip hers as Mom walks out. Good timing.

"You've got one cool kid here, Dr. Santos," Avery says.

"I do," Mom says as we walk away. "Kaia, what was that about?"

"You know... college talk."

Tatang's not the only one with surprises.

● ● ●

After we get home I run upstairs. A couple of big boxes sit outside Tatang's door, one marked *Give* and the other labeled *Ship*.

"Tatang? You in there?" I shout into his room, but there's no answer. The door's open but I don't see him inside.

I peek into the Give box and pull out a handful of his prized shirts. There's one with lobsters in cooking pots and another with Santa Clauses wearing sunglasses and hula skirts. Why's he donating them? He loves these.

"Whatcha doing?" Tatang says. I drop the clothes and spin around. He rests his hand on my shoulder. "Sorry, anak, I didn't mean to startle you."

"Are you giving your collection away?"

He shrugs. "I don't want to take so many things home with me. Best to start simple."

"But these are your favorites."

"Like I always say, they're just *things*."

I close the lid and follow him into his bedroom. What else is he getting rid of?

Then I see: the empty bookshelves, the bare walls where his framed photos hung.

"Care to help me finish packing?" he asks.

"What's left to pack?" He flashes a smile and I try to return it, but it feels too forced. "Tatang, how come you've never told me any war stories?"

He sits in his reading chair. "I can share some now. Did I spark some questions after your mom's lecture?"

I nod. "A few."

"Fantastic. What are they?"

"Do you . . . do you remember your military service number?"

He looks at me in surprise, then gives a great big belly laugh. "How about an easier question to start with? Like the day I enlisted for the war?"

"Sure." I sit on the bed.

"I presented myself at Fort McKinley with a brave face, even though inside I felt the opposite, but I wanted to serve my country. . . ."

We go back and forth with more questions and answers: how scared he felt, how he did it because he wanted to defend his homeland from fascism, how those hard times changed him. "They made me stronger."

I thought that leaving his home here might be difficult for Tatang, but I see now that his life has been full of changes that he had to figure out—and he always did. Maybe that's why he makes moving seem like it's no big deal, because with everything else he's lived through, it's not.

As Tatang goes on, I glance over his shoulder to the naked wall. We're so close to the finish line on our movie. Soon I'll be able to help him put everything back where it belongs.

19

Editing time. Almost there.

Abby and I take over one of the edit bays at camp, a dark little room with monitors and equipment.

I plug the camera into a computer, download our shots, and pull everything up on screen. It pauses on a still of Trey as Bakunawa walking along the shore, the sunlight framing his handsome face.

We fast forward and freeze on the cafeteria scene where Bakunawa's getting chased away by the other creatures. Trey's mouth is open in fright and Dave, Jalissa, and Jackson wave their arms, pots and spoons raised.

Abby presses play. The scene moves on . . . only there's no sound.

"Wait a second," Abby says, scrolling the scene back. She clicks more buttons and plays it again but still there's no audio, like it's on mute. We can see Dave screaming his one line but can't hear anything.

I press rewind and turn the volume all the way up. "Why isn't it working?"

Abby clicks on the mouse frantically. Her brow moves into a deep V.

"Oh no. No, no, no..."

"We're probably forgetting something really basic," I say. I walk to the door, peek my head out, and spot Eliza. I wave her over and explain.

"Let's take a look." Eliza picks up the camera. "Oh, dear."

"What? What is it?" Abby asks.

Eliza points to a label: *Camera 2*.

"This one has a dead microphone. Another group turned in a technical report but they must have forgotten to take the camera out of the equipment room or put up a sign so no one else could use it. I'm so sorry, girls. You're not hearing audio because you didn't record any."

"Are you kidding me?" Abby drops her head.

"Could we ... could we add the sound in post?" I suggest, but Abby groans. She turns to me with her saddest face.

"This is all my fault—I didn't test the camera before we started shooting that day. That's the biggest rookie mistake. What kind of director does that?"

"Hey, it happens," Eliza says.

I remember something Tatang told me. I repeat it slowly, trying to get the words right: "Maysa a bullalayaw isu masansan, imaetangan iti langit kaano iti init aglawag kalpasan dayta no adda iti tudo."

I don't know a lot of Ilocano, but I think I got this one right.

"That sounds lovely, Kaia. What does it mean?" Eliza asks.

"A rainbow is often seen when the sun shines just after it has rained."

"And this has to do with my dumb mistake how?" Abby says.

"It's something Tatang says—when things get hard they always get better. We'll try again. Don't worry, Abbs, you're doing amazing. You're the reason we've gotten this far." I pat her shoulder.

Eventually Abby gives us a half smile. "It's tough being a perfectionist."

"Sounds like you girls know exactly what next steps to take," Eliza says.

Eliza leaves, and Abby scrolls through our soundless footage again. I'm trying to stay positive, but she says what I'm really thinking.

"We're never going to finish on time now."

• • •

Abby and Trey come home with me after camp so we can figure out what to do next. One week left. We still have to cut everything together, and I have no idea how we'll shoot a new cafeteria scene by then.

We sit at the pool's edge, dangling our legs into the water.

Dad comes out of his office and sits with us. "How did editing go?"

Abby sighs. "It didn't."

"I thought making our film would be more fun than this," Trey says.

"How so?" Dad asks.

"We were *so close*, but now we have to film the whole cafeteria scene all over—we had no audio. It seems impossible now," Abby says, shaking her head. Dad listens carefully. One thing I love about my dad is he never makes me think anything I say is unimportant. Lainey's like him that way.

"We should just forget about the contest." Abby said this? My eyes go wide.

"Maybe you're right," Trey says. "It takes so long to get the makeup on and we'll need Dave and Jalissa and Jackson and everyone back to help, but they're too busy finishing their own movies."

I glare at them. "You want to give up?"

"I feel for you kids. And I wonder…" Dad says. "You want to come to the studio on Saturday? Whenever I'm stuck I get inspired by seeing other peoples' art. It's a weekend, so you wouldn't be able to work at camp anyway. Spend your day cooking up solutions."

We glance at each other. Dad's taken us to work before and we've always had a blast, but I'm not sure we can spare any time away from our movie.

Abby perks up. "Sounds like a plan."

Trey says, "I'm in."

"Only one person left to hear from," Dad says.

Maybe he's right. A new brain spark would do us good.

"Are you buying us lunch at the commissary?" I ask.

He crosses his heart. "Deal."

"I would have come even without that," I say.

"Perfecto! Abby and Trey, I'll call your parents to see if that'd be okay. And tell you grommets what: Our families haven't gotten together in a while, so when we're back from the studio we can do my favorite thing." Dad gets up and ties on the apron he bought for himself that Lainey and I begged him not to get because we knew he'd never take it off: *May the Forks Be With You.* "I love a good Filipino barbecue!"

20

Going to Dad's office always feels like an adventure.

A wide black metal gate greets us, and Dad rolls his car window down to scan a card. The gates swing open and Abby, Trey, and I wave to the security guard, who waves back.

We park and take an elevator that brings us into Dad's building. A studio has hundreds of people at work, from security guards to animators like Dad to the pastry chef at the commissary who makes the most delicious pies. Dad always sneaks extra slices to take home.

As we walk in I see my future: I'm head of a makeup effects department for big blockbuster movies. Mom and Dad and Toby will visit during lunchtime, and on the weekends I'll travel with my crew to places like Paris and the Sahara Desert. Abby will direct and Trey will star. Then one day we'll visit Camp Art Attack as grown-ups, carry around our Oscars, and remember where it all started. Abby calls this our "origin story."

We follow Dad to a floor of cubicles and offices with glass walls.

It's quiet and somewhat dark; they keep it this way for the animators. A few people are in the office today, working. As we walk I peek into different cubbies and catch glimpses of what's on peoples' screens: a fiery storm, a monster eating a troll, a log bridge that collapses into a river because of the monster eating the troll.

"Awesome," Abby whispers to me.

This feels like a place where we need to whisper because everyone's focusing, although some people notice us and wave. One says, "Hey, Kaia and crew!"

Dad's space looks like The Cave at home, with a big desk, computer screens, and a bookshelf crammed with papers.

"Want to see what I'm working on?"

On the screen is a volcano he designed. He clicks his mouse and the volcano erupts. *Pow!*

"How'd you get it to do that?" Trey asks.

"Magic!" Dad laughs. "Come on, let's explore."

We walk down more hallways and finally head onto a long bridge that connects one building to another. We stop to look at the lot below. Everything's moving—people and props and golf carts.

Dad waves us forward. "Keep going, gang. We have an appointment."

"For what?" I ask, but he just smiles and walks fast.

We take another elevator down—this place is a huge maze! As it opens, we step into sunlight and onto the backlot.

Finally, where all the action happens.

Everywhere we turn there's something fun. A group of actors dressed like clowns passes our way. I make eye contact with one and she tips her three-foot-tall hat. A golf cart of women and men in suits honks at us. Crates of fake boulders are rolled across the street as huge lights are set up on an outdoor stage.

"I love it here," Trey says.

We walk past soundstages with elephant doors—they're called that because they need to be wide enough for elephants to fit through!—and red wigwag lights on the outside, some of them flashing, which means somewhere inside they're filming and they want everyone near to be quiet.

We round the corner and enter a street of cafés and shops like we're in downtown LA—only when you look behind the buildings, you see that they're just façades with nothing behind them.

A woman in a bright orange safety vest holds out her hand to stop us from going any farther.

Dad turns to us and puts a finger up to his nose.

A director shouts: "Action!"

Out of nowhere, a stunt person drops from high above onto a puffy blue mat as a camera dollies to get the shot.

"And cut!" the director yells. My friends and I grin at each other. The crossing guard motions us along, like it's nothing. Typical day.

• • •

We reach a row of white portable trailers.

"Kaia, I think you'll like this," Dad says with a sly smile as he knocks on the door.

"Oh my gosh… someone famous?" Abby asks.

A woman opens the door. She's around my parents' age, with short, spiky black hair and a warm smile. "Hey, everybody, come on in. I've been waiting for you!"

We step up into a room lined with red vinyl barbershop chairs, huge mirrors on the walls, and one wall covered with Polaroid pictures of different kinds of characters: bald aliens, hairy bigfoots, enchanting fairies. In the middle sits a long table overflowing with makeup tools and bins. I'm drooling.

"Kids," Dad says, "I'd like you to meet Flora Yamada. She's head of makeup effects on the film I'm working on."

"Kaia, I hear we have a lot in common," she says.

I feel a little shy at first because I can't believe we're here. Then I blurt: "I want your job!"

She chuckles. "Then you'll have to learn more about what I do, right? Let's start by naming a character and figuring out some physical traits to re-create."

Abby and Trey shout out: Frankenstein! A mummy! Dracula!

"How about… a bakunawa?" Dad says.

"Oh yeah, I heard all about your film. I hope I can see it," Flora says.

Abby nods. "Definitely."

"What do you think, Kaia? Any of those sound good?" Flora asks.

Not really. I want to try something different from what we've been working on. "Hmm ... how about ... the manananggal?" Dad smiles at me. "She's a Filipino creature, vampire-like with huge bat wings and a long tongue, who can split her body in two," I say. "Then she eats people." Everyone laughs.

"The manananggal it is." Flora points out which supplies to grab. She quickly creates one, then demonstrates how to do all kinds of effects, like bags under our eyes and scars on our cheeks. We take pictures as we try on dentures of razor-sharp teeth and squeeze red liquid makeup that looks like real blood onto our arms. Dad pops in purple contact lenses and we shriek before exploding in laughter.

"Kaia, why don't you pick out a specific effect for all of us to try?" Flora says.

"A flesh wound?" I say.

Trey works on Abby and I work on Dad while Flora works on herself. Flora makes it seem easy. I grab a silicone piece and try to stick it to Dad's cheek but it won't stay put—no matter what I do, it droops, then falls off.

My hands shake as I try to make it work. I want to show I can do this.

"Here," Flora says, moving the piece around and trying to help me figure out how to fit it on. "Sometimes you have to test all kinds of different ideas to find the best solution." It won't stick for her either, so she leaves the piece hanging as is. I decide to glue a zipper on top of the piece and fill it in with paint, so now it looks like a chunk of skin is bursting out of the metal teeth.

"Gross!" Abby says, and Trey screams.

At the end of the session we stand shoulder to shoulder, three regular old flesh-eating Filipino vampires.

Flora holds up an instant camera and Dad takes our picture with her in the middle. He takes a few more and hands one to each of us. Flora tacks her square onto the wall. We're officially official.

Our studio day ends at the commissary. Perfect.

The commissary's a huge cafeteria with different stations, like Burger Bar, Donut Wall, Bibimbap Bowls, and (my favorite) Nacho Boats.

"Grab a tray, load up, and meet me back at that corner table," Dad says, and we scatter.

Over lunch we share ideas of how to fix our soundless footage—and we try some fried crickets, too. (Crunchy and salty!)

Dad was right. We needed this day.

• • •

At home my friends and I run up to my room and hop onto my bed. Abby closes her eyes and Trey swipes through his phone; we're quiet and in our own thoughts. That's how I know we're connected—we can be together, but separate.

I text Avery:

When do you think we'll hear back about the application?

We've texted a bunch of times now and I'm crossing all

my fingers we'll make something happen. Avery helped me find out that Mom *did* know about the law passed to recognize Filipino veterans—but she's been way too busy to do anything about it.

My phone dings as I press send.

Abby sits up. "I want a dad like yours."

She's never met her father, and even though her mom calls him a deadbeat, Abby secretly hopes one day they'll meet so she can decide for herself. Abby's mom is a supermom—two parents in one—but sometimes I feel bad Abby doesn't have a dad too, because I'm grateful for how amazing mine is.

I hug her, then smack her lightly with a pillow. We giggle.

Trey yanks the pillow away. "Okay, don't get mad, but I've been thinking about something."

"Uh-oh," Abby says. "Does that mean your head hurts?" She and I crack up.

"No, I'm being serious. I was thinking about the contest. What if… what if we don't place?"

Abby holds her hands up to our faces. "Stop it right there. We need to think big. Only. Positive. Thoughts."

She's right.

"I know we stand a chance," I say.

"Of course we do," Abby says.

"Yeah," Trey says, "but there's not a single middle-schooler in LA who's into film who's not entering. A ton of eighth grad-ers and even high-schoolers. My parents were watching the news and they did a story about all the kids making their beach movies. Some of them go to fancy schools where they use *real* cameras *with film*. All we have is makeup. Excellent lizard makeup."

I shoot him a look.

"Yeah, we did a great job but we should still prepare for the worst, right?" he says.

Abby nods and raises her eyebrows at me: she's saying he has a point. And maybe he does, but I don't want to think about it.

Trey turns some music on from my laptop and we settle back down.

I scroll through our soundless shots on my phone, and weirdly they play in time to the song that's on. It makes our footage feel like a music video.

"Abbs, listen—look." I hand her my phone. Flora said to find solutions, that we have to try everything. Maybe we don't need to reshoot after all. "We could use music!"

"Let me see that," Abby says. "You might be on to something...."

Trey sits up and watches over Abby's shoulder. "Kaia!" We all glance at each other. This could work—we might have a fix for our soundless footage.

"Yes! Good thinking," Abby says.

The doorbell rings and voices float up to my room.

"My parents," Trey says.

The doorbell rings again and this time we hear Abby's mom, and Uncle Roy, too.

A knock on my door.

"Come in." It's Mom and Toby. He runs inside and climbs onto the bed with us.

"I have a surprise for you all," Mom says, her eyes lit up. "Follow me."

● ● ●

Downstairs, Trey hoists Toby onto his back. They yank on an imaginary whistle and shout: "Chooo-chooooo!"

We walk toward the backyard, where Tatang and our parents sit under the trees and twinkle lights. It's starting to darken and a few stars brighten the sky.

Look up. What do you see? Tatang's voice in my head.

I spot Mom's surprise on the patio—our dining table! It has an incredible centerpiece. Instead of place mats and silverware, large wide blades of shiny banana leaves cover the top and a glorious meal sits on the leaves: small mounds of white rice, sweet fried bananas, slices of savory seasoned meat, and whole shrimp with the heads still on. Mangoes cut into grids and folded out like flowers dot the table.

"Boodle fight!" I shout.

"A poodle what?" Abby asks, and my family laughs.

"I hope everyone's hands are clean," Tatang says. "If not, wash up, then please take a seat."

After we wash, Dad helps Toby into his booster chair and

we each find a place. I sit next to Tatang. He's wearing a shirt with plates, knives, and forks on it.

"I thought you were giving all your shirts away?" I ask.

He tugs at it. "I'm hanging on to a few, like this one, because I always need good dinner attire... and the one with the popcorn buckets because it reminds me of when we watch movies together."

I grin. I'll bet he's saving it for walking the red carpet with me.

Once everyone is seated, Tatang says, "Kaia, before our guests think we're rude not to pass out utensils, would you care to explain?"

"Sure. A boodle fight is an old Philippine military style of eating when soldiers ate with their hands—it's also called kamayan style. First they'd wash with jugs of water, then they'd dig right in."

"That's where the *fight* part comes from," Mom says. "They'd 'attack' the food, kind of a free-for-all until every last grain of rice disappeared."

"Although I prefer to think of it less as a fight and more as a humble feast with loved ones," Tatang adds.

"Were you in the war, Tatang?" asks Eric, Trey's dad.

He nods. "One of the two hundred fifty thousand Filipino soldiers who fought in World War II." I think the parents want to hear more, but he says, "We have all night for stories. Please, let's eat first."

"No plates?" Trey says.

"Nope. No plates and no utensils, only your appetite," Dad says.

Tatang goes in first, scooping up a bit of rice with some meat, and we all follow.

It's so different to eat without forks and spoons, your fingertips feeling food before your taste buds do. I look around the table, and even though everyone seemed a little awkward at first, they're all enjoying themselves now.

"How was today?" asks Vanessa, Trey's mom.

We three leap in and tell them about the studio visit and the film so far. The grown-ups ask tons of questions.

At the end of our meal Sam says, "Santos family, this was amazing."

Mom passes out wipes and says, "I'm so glad everyone could join us. We wanted to get in at least one last boodle fight before Tatang's trip." She looks at me and smiles.

I had hoped no one would bring that up.

"We heard your news, Tatang. We'll miss seeing you," Eric says.

"Don't worry, we're not letting him go without a proper party first," Mom says. "You'll be getting an invite soon."

"And I'll be making the cake!" Uncle Roy says.

• • •

After everyone's gone, I'm in my room and there's a buzzing on my desk. I grab my phone, hoping to see Lainey, but it's Avery:

Haven't heard anything yet . . . don't stress!

Avery reminds me a little of Lainey—they both seem to know about everything. Although spending time with Flora at the studio made me realize that I know a few things now, too.

It's all coming together.

21

Last day of postproduction. This is it. We've reached the deadline.

I sit with Trey and Abby in the edit bay at camp and we watch our movie. It ends with bloopers from when Trey plops into the cake—the best ending ever. We've watched that scene at least fifty times and even Trey thinks it's hilarious now.

Dad's idea of finding inspiration at the studio worked. Instead of trying to reshoot our scene, we cut everything together, added catchy music, and turned that part into a montage where we didn't need the original audio. It was hard work to finish everything on time, but now we have an amazing project to enter.

Inside I'm fireworks, but I say, "Not too shabby."

"We're... pretty dang awesome," Abby says, equally calm.

We look at each other ... and happy-scream at the top of our lungs.

Trey and I jump up and do a silly dance and Abby takes our picture before she stares back at the computer screen.

"Should I?" Abby asks.

"Do it," Trey says.

"Yup. No turning back now," I say.

Abby types something and attaches a file. "Ten grand . . . limo ride . . . entry into a film workshop next year . . . Okay, here goes nothin' . . ."

She covers her eyes with one hand and hovers over the mouse with the other. We pile our hands on top of hers.

"Three . . . two . . . one . . . send!" Trey shouts. We aim and click the button.

Poof! Into the internet galaxy it goes.

An auto-reply pings back:

Thank you for your submission to the youth category of the Beach Season Film Festival. Please expect to hear back from our submission committee within two weeks.

22

"How high can we make them, Kai-Kai?" Toby's little voice squeaks out as we build a tower of blocks on the kitchen floor. He piles one more onto the top and it teeters over, crashing to the tile in bright yellows, blues, and reds. He wails.

"We just have to try it again," I tell him.

"I want the tower now!" he shouts.

I know how he feels. It feels like a year since we sent off our movie and I can't take it much longer. Eliza said we'll probably hear after this weekend. Waiting's as painful as stepping into cold air after a warm swim.

My parents and Uncle Roy hang out with me and Toby while we wait for Tatang to finish getting ready. Today is our Share Bears brunch.

Mom's staring at the wall calendar and I catch her worried look. I see why: the days are full of Xs and getting closer to the big red circle around Tatang's goodbye date. So far Eliza hasn't gotten any updates about the festival, but we have to get in. We have no other option.

Mom folds her arms and gives a little sigh. "Where should we eat?"

"Let's have Tatang choose," Dad says.

"I'll get him," Uncle Roy says. He cups his mouth and yells: "Tataaaaang!" Uncle and I burst out laughing, but of course Mom scolds us with a look.

"Roy, can you please be a grown-up?" she says, and he hides behind me.

Tatang rushes down the stairs. "My goodness, none of you are on Filipino time! Nice job, family!"

"As a punctual person, I am completely offended by that," Uncle Roy says.

"Tatang, where do you want to go for brunch?" Dad asks as he hoists Toby onto his back.

"Ah, an important question for one of our last family meals together . . . at least until I can get back to visit." I wish he didn't have to put it that way. "But I'm thinking we should brunch *after* our outing."

"What outing?" Dad asks.

Tatang waves a sheet of paper in the air. "I have a surprise. Someone start up the minivan, please. I've downloaded our tickets."

• • •

We pack into the van and Dad types an address that Tatang gives him into the car's GPS. We drive along the ocean and

I spot surfers bobbing on the water, their silhouettes dark against the midday sun.

"Okay, spill it, dude. Where are we going?" Uncle Roy asks, but Tatang won't give any clues.

The GPS says "destination reached" as we roll up to a big stucco building with no sign or windows. We look at each other, confused.

"Care to tell us now, Tatang?" Mom says.

"We're going flying," he says.

"Excuse me?"

"Flying. Skydiving."

Uncle Roy and I make eye contact and start to laugh.

"Wow!" says Dad. "Sounds good to me."

Flying! So that's what Tatang meant on his journal list: *Learn to fly.*

"We can't go *skydiving*," Mom says.

"Don't worry, it's all indoors," Tatang says.

Her face gets twisty. Uncle Roy says, "Sis, look how excited he is," and the two of them start arguing about whether we should go inside. Whenever they get this way I imagine them as little kids.

"Joy, Roy, please," Tatang says, but they don't listen. "Children!" he booms. Tatang places a hand to his heart like it hurts him to shout. This quiets them. Now he's the one who looks annoyed. "Before we go in, I want you to close your eyes."

"For once can we not do this?" Mom says. "Can we please just get some breakfast?"

"Close. Your. Eyes," Tatang says in his sternest voice.

The adults do as he asks. Tatang closes his too but I secretly keep mine open. I want to see what he's plotting.

"Good. Now feel whatever you're feeling—frustration, humor, sadness—and let that emotion be." Mom keeps huffing but with her eyes shut. Everyone else seems soothed by Tatang's voice. "Whatever you're feeling, it will pass." Tatang pauses. "Now, think of your happiest moment. Hold it in your head."

A strange thing happens. Uncle Roy has a little smile on his face, Tatang a big one, and even Mom looks like she's remembering something good. "I want you to understand that this is the gift of memory. No matter what you're feeling you can recall the good, any time you want. Now think of the wonderful things ahead. What do you most want for yourself and for your loved ones? Are you ready? Open your eyes."

They do.

"All right, look around and see the good in this moment. Our health, happiness, and each other. We just time-traveled. Did you like that?"

Mom goes back to frowning. "I love you, Tatang, but I'm not in the mood."

It's Tatang who sighs now. "I'm trying to help you, anak. How will you all handle things when I am away?"

"Then maybe you shouldn't go." If no one else will say it, I will.

"You know, I've been thinking, Tatang . . . ," Mom says.

"What if you do a test run? After Christmas we can reassess whether you really want to make the move a permanent one."

"That's a great idea!" I say.

But Tatang only looks at us with kind eyes. He takes my brother's hand. "How about we all go in and enjoy this. Please? For the old dude?"

Mom buries her face in her hands, but this time she groan-laughs. "Fine, fine."

"You heard Big T," says Uncle Roy. "Let's go in and fly." He slides the door open as wide as it will go.

● ● ●

"Are you sure this is safe?" Mom asks.

"It's not hard. Children as young as six can do it. Although, sorry, Toby, you'll have to sit this one out and watch," Tatang says.

Uncle Roy grabs the tickets from Tatang and hands them to the front desk guy.

We spend the next half hour getting trained. "You'll be experiencing the thrill of free fall but without jumping from a plane," the instructor says.

Mom's still not into this, but she listens.

After the session we get outfitted in bright blue jumpsuits, goggles, and helmets. We take one look at each other, and everyone cracks up—even Mom and Toby. The trainer gave him goggles to wear too. Mom's eyes tear up from laughing so much and I wonder if Tatang planned it this way.

The trainer leads us into "the fly room," with a huge clear, vertical cylinder and benches all around. We're about to sky-dive in a giant tall wind tunnel. I'm not scared like with the roller coaster—riding that showed me I can get over my nerves.

"Who's first?" the trainer asks.

"Joy? You want to try?" Tatang says.

Her eyes widen. "Someone else, please."

"You can do it, Mom," I say, but she shakes her head.

"Kaia?" Tatang says to me. I kind of want to go first, but I know how much he's been waiting for this; it's on his list, after all.

"I think you should kick us off," I say.

"Great, because I'm ready!"

"Good man," the trainer says, and together they head into the tube.

Tatang's smile is gigantic—mine too.

The instructor counts down and Tatang shoots into the air, his arms suspended like wings. Toby smushes his nose up against the glass and Tatang waves at him.

I feel butterflies for my great-grandpa getting to do something like this. They're the same ones I feel about tomorrow: at camp my group will get to hear our names announced.

Mom walks up to the cylinder and stares in awe. I know she's holding this feeling, this moment in her head like I am: the most wonderful thing, my great-grandfather, flying.

23

Monday morning! I bound down the stairs in my favorite sundress, and as soon as Tatang sees me he says, "Today's your big day!"

I pat a fast drumroll on my thighs.

"Kaia, let's remember that there are lots of kids entering the festival. I don't want you to get your hopes up too high, okay?" Mom says in her professor voice.

"Besides, your group won no matter what the results are," Tatang says, even though the glint in his eyes matches mine.

• • •

The opening camp bell chimes. I dash into class and sink into a beanbag. Eliza's happy and humming while she gathers her things, so I know this means excellent news. She turns my way with a huge smile.

I knew it!

Noisy chatter fills the room. I'll have to not seem too

braggy around the groups that don't make it in when she gives us the good news—they worked hard too. I don't want anyone to feel bad.

Eliza sits in a beanbag and scans her clipboard.

"I can't take it anymore. Tell us who won!" Dave Conway calls out.

Abby looks at me and makes her eyes go wide.

My heart feels like it's going to beat out of my chest. "Well?"

Eliza looks at me then down at her list—her smile disappears.

Oh no.

"I'm so very sorry, everyone, but no teams from Camp Art Attack were announced as winners."

"Seriously?" Trey says. "Not even mine?"

The class grumbles. Abby buries her face in her hands.

I can't believe it. "But we all worked so hard."

"You did," Eliza says. "Okay, everyone, real talk. I know this is disappointing, but that's how things go sometimes. I've learned this from whenever I audition for something or go on a job interview—you win some and you lose some. It doesn't change the fact that you made amazing art, and we're going to celebrate! We'll premiere your movies at the end of camp and invite your families to walk our very own red carpet. What do you think?"

I think she expected this would get a round of applause, but the room is quiet.

"That's not really the same," Abby says.

"You're sure they didn't choose any of our movies?" I ask, and Eliza nods.

My eyes water, but I try not to let any tears break free. So this is a broken heart. I have to tell Tatang that I failed.

• • •

After camp ends, Trey, Abby, and I go outside. Trey stuffs his hands into his pockets and kicks a few pebbles. Abby pulls a camera to her eye but stops. She sighs. "This feels like a bad dream."

"Like the first time I didn't get cast as Peter Pan," Trey says. He gets rejected a lot after auditions, and his parents tell him he has the choice to stop, but he always decides to keep going. Normally he shrugs and tells me and Abby: *You win some, you lose some,* like Eliza told us. Now I understand how much it hurts.

"I'm sorry, Kaia. I know you wanted this for Tatang," Abby tells me.

I want to say something to make them feel better, but I can't think of a single thing.

We walk in silence. After a few blocks I see the red tiled roof and palm trees of Ocean Gardens. I pause in front of the gates.

Not only will I have to tell my family the awful news, but Tatang will have to break it to everyone here. They were rooting for us.

"You guys want to go in? Maybe that'll cheer us up," I suggest.

Abby says, "Sure. I've always wanted to meet your friends here."

At the front desk the staff gives us visitor badges that we hook onto our shirts. Cynthia and a few other residents wave and come over.

My friends meet, young and old.

"Where's Harold?" I ask.

"Probably resting. I think he said he was feeling a little under the weather," Cynthia says.

"What are you all up to?" I say.

"We're about to have tea on the roof deck ... and you're coming with!"

We follow them into an elevator that opens onto a rooftop covered in fake grass with lounge chairs and a view of the ocean.

"Wow, this is living," Abby says, pulling her camera out and getting some shots.

One of the ladies offers us tea and we sit. Trey takes his cup. His pinky springs up and he delicately slurps, making everyone laugh.

I look out at the wide ocean and start to feel the tiniest bit better. I'm glad we stopped by.

"Kaia, how's the movie going? Celestino said you should hear the results soon," Cynthia says.

Trey and Abby glance at me. "We lost," I say. My eyes sting and I can feel tears wanting to come out.

Cynthia touches my shoulder. "I'm so sorry, kids."

"I am too. I wanted a lot of people to see our movie," Trey says.

"They still will, won't they?" Cynthia asks.

"Not at a big fancy premiere," Abby says. "I even had my dress picked out."

"Tatang's going to be so disappointed," I say.

I begin to cry—it gets Abby going, too.

"Oh dear," Cynthia says. She hugs both of us and others pat our shoulders.

I wipe my face, take a deep breath, and straighten up in my chair. Maybe I can still fix things.

"Do you think . . . ," I say. "Do you think you can help me convince Tatang not to move? He listens to all of you."

Cynthia takes a sip of her tea and looks out at the view, then back at me. "I'm so sorry, Kaia, but I don't think Celestino will change his mind. It sounds like he's had this plan for many years."

What was I even thinking, asking them that? I've stopped crying but my chest feels heavy. I still have to go home and tell Tatang that we lost.

"I'd love it if you three would show us your movie." One of the ladies leans forward. "We'll make a night of it in the media room."

I try to return her smile. "That's a good idea," I say, and we finish up our tea in silence.

After, Abby asks the group: "Can we take a picture—with our teacups—to remember the moment?"

Abby poses everyone in front of the railing, the beach behind, the light hitting our faces. She grabs a portable tripod from her camera bag, sets everything up, and runs back over. "Okay, teacups and pinkies up!"

Everyone laughs. It feels good to do that.

I focus my gaze on the water again. I'll have to disappoint my whole family, after all they did to help me. How will I break the news?

• • •

I take as long as I can to walk home and try to play Tatang's noticing game to get my mind off things, but it's too hard.

The front door's unlocked so I slip in as quietly as I can. I'm greeted with helium balloons in ocean colors and a vase of fluffy white and blue flowers on the dining table. There's even a homemade sign: *CONGRATULATIONS B IS FOR BAKUNAWA!*

It's a party but with nothing to celebrate.

I sprint to the stairs—maybe Tatang won't see me—but out of nowhere he rushes in my direction with his arms flung out.

"Well?" The smile lines pop around his eyes. The look he's giving me—it's the exact one I pictured for this moment. He's even wearing a fancy Hawaiian shirt, like he was waiting to celebrate.

I don't know what to say.

I want to tell him that we lost. Instead my lips turn up in a frozen smile.

"Tatang, I—"

His face softens. "Everything okay, anak?"

Tell him, Kaia.

"My group and I... well... we're really excited about the red carpet premiere."

I can't even do this part right.

I'm not sure what he's thinking because I keep my eyes focused on my feet.

"I'm getting ready to meet Harold. How about joining us? On the way you can tell me more."

"Okay," I say.

24

We walk, slowly. Tatang looked so excited a few minutes ago but his face has turned more serious. He hangs his arm around my shoulder. "You're pretty quiet. Everything okay?"

Tell him now, Kaia.

I try to find my strength but I'm too embarrassed. I wish I could burrow into a hole and never come out.

"Sorry, it's just that I... I'm a little tired."

He smiles at me. "I'm a good listener."

For the briefest moment I look up at him and we make eye contact—but I turn away. "Not right now. Can we... just walk?"

Luckily, Tatang doesn't say another word. We reach the spot where he'll meet Harold, in front of a grand old brick hotel not far from the water.

"Tatang, I do have something to tell you," I say, but his phone rings.

"Sorry, anak, let me get this. Harold must be running late." He puts his phone to his ear.

After. I'll tell him after his call.

"Is it okay if I wait in the lobby?" I ask, and he nods.

Whenever my parents and I pass this building we take a quick walk inside. It's the neatest place. I step in and look at the fireplaces and chandeliers, plush chairs and couches.

Tatang appears by my side. "Harold's got a cold so we'll walk with him another time. The good news is that now I'm all ears." He puts his hand on my shoulder and peers at me.

"All righty, now lean your heads together, please!" says a woman nearby, holding a camera to her face. She reminds me a little of an older version of Abby.

I point over to the couple getting photographed. "Look, it's a Filipino wedding."

Tatang says, "How lovely!"

The bride has blond hair swept up and topped with a flowing veil, and the groom has darker skin like mine and a face that seems familiar. That's how I feel whenever I meet other Filipinos, as if we're connected, because even though I don't know them, I know some things about the place where we came from.

We can tell it's a Filipino wedding because of the traditional shirt some of the men are wearing. It's called a barong, made from thin, ivory-colored fabric. Tatang, Uncle Roy, and Dad each have one that they wear to weddings and other family celebrations.

The photographer snaps away while a frantic woman flits around the lobby clapping her hands and telling people to enter the ballroom for the mother-son dance. A gold badge pinned to her dress says *Wedding Coordinator*.

"We're starting soon!" She grabs Tatang's elbow.

I'm about to tell her we're not with the wedding when Tatang says, "Why, thank you." He gives me a secret smile, and we get pulled into another elegant room. Tatang and I stand in the back, looking at tables of people and flowers and champagne glasses.

"Tatang, we can't be here," I whisper.

"It's okay, we won't stay. I love weddings. I just want to take one look."

Everyone clinks their forks against glasses for the bride and groom to kiss. An emcee announces the mother-son dance and the groom and his mother take the floor.

A weird thought pops into my brain. If I ever get married, will Tatang be there?

We watch people leave their tables to dance. Tatang taps me on the shoulder.

"May I have this dance?"

"I don't know how to dance like that."

"It's easy, just move to the music. Like this." Tatang lifts my hands and places one on his shoulder and the other in his hand. We sway in circles.

I close my eyes. If I ever get married, I'll remember this moment.

"Yoo-hoo! This way!" says the photographer, the camera flashing as we both look at her.

We bust up. I take Tatang's arm and we run all the way through the lobby back into the summer sun.

Outside, we're still laughing. I want to keep this feeling forever.

A woman holding shopping bags waves at us. As she gets closer, I realize it's Eliza.

"I thought that was you, Kaia." She puts her bags down and juts a hand toward Tatang. "Hi, I'm Eliza Rodriguez, one of Kaia's camp motivators. You must be her great-grandfather I've heard so much about."

"A pleasure to meet you," he says in his most charming way. "Kaia and her team did an excellent job."

"They knocked it out of the park with their movie, that's for sure," she says. "Nice to run into you both. I'll see you soon, Kaia." Eliza walks away, shouting, "Gotta get going with my retail therapy!"

"What great spirit your teacher has," he says.

I take a huge breath. "Tatang, we didn't place in the contest."

He tilts my chin up so that our eyes meet. "What happened, Kaia?"

"We lost, but I was too scared to tell you."

"Oh, anak, I thought that's what happened. Harold confirmed it when we talked." I can tell by his sad smile that he's disappointed. "Truly, it's okay," he says, "but why would you not be honest with me right away? That's not how I taught you."

"I wanted you to have something to feel excited about with me like you do with Lainey."

"Is that what's worrying you?" Tatang pulls me into a hug.

"You and your friends created something meaningful for people to enjoy no matter the outcome. That's what I call winning."

"You don't need to try to make me feel better."

"My dear, there are many things in my own life I wish had turned out differently, but I'm grateful for those too. They all taught me something about myself."

"I guess."

"Tell you what, let's still go for that walk. You'll feel much better."

"Can we please head home now?"

He nods. He puts a warm hand into mine and we go.

• • •

I lost, and now Tatang will leave with this as one of his last LA memories.

Mom walks into the house with Toby, fresh from daycare with finger paint smeared all over his clothes. "Kai-Kai!" He runs to me. His sweetness makes me forget everything until I notice Mom carrying two large, flat boxes. We always order pizza for celebrations.

"I got your favorite, sweetie—barbecue chicken pizza, no onions," she sings out. "Well? Did you hear yet?"

I don't want to make the same mistake like with Tatang. "Do you mind if I save the bad news for when we eat?" I don't want to have to repeat my story to Dad and Uncle Roy, too. I'd rather get it over with all at once.

Instead of giving Mom a chance to react, I run upstairs to hide out until dinner. She doesn't force me to come down to set the table.

A little later I hear voices from below. Everyone's home.

There's a knock on my door. "Kaia, time to eat. Come and join us, honey," Dad says through the door.

Everyone's seated, pizza boxes open and my celebration bouquet as the centerpiece. We pass around the salad bowl. No one's asking me any questions or mentioning Beach Season.

"We didn't get chosen for the festival," I force myself to say. "Sorry." I bite into my slice and stare at my plate, trying not to cry again.

"Oh, sweetheart," Mom says. "Whether you made it in doesn't matter. You still did a terrific job."

"Exactly. And you learned so much," Dad says.

Uncle Roy waves his hands around with a huff. "Those judges don't know a single thing about movies!"

"I don't want to talk about it anymore, if that's okay," I say, and Tatang squeezes my shoulder.

Mom's phone rings from the other room. She gets up for it and jets back in. "It's Lainey!"

"Elena!" Tatang beams at Lainey's face on the screen.

At least now they'll talk about her instead of me.

"We're having dinner right now and celebrating Kaia," Mom says.

"Yeah, she made the best film for camp," Uncle Roy says.

"Kaia wrote it and did all the makeup and costumes," Dad says. "She's got some good pictures to show you."

"Wow, that's so exciting Kai-Kai!" Lainey says. Lainey asks me about my movie—not once does my family ask her about her trip.

"Can I please talk to her?" I ask Mom. She rubs my arm and hands me the phone.

I have so much to tell my sister.

"Is it … is it okay if I go to my room?"

My parents nod. I run all the way upstairs.

For who knows how long, Lainey and I catch up, filling each other in on all the time we've spent apart, starting with the contest.

"I loved seeing all the pictures from your movie," she says. I've missed her voice. It perks me up. "Guess what?" Lainey says. "I got you some cool souvenirs."

"Is one of them a state-of-the-art digital clock?" I ask, and she busts up.

"What?"

"You'll see when you get home," I say.

"How about I send you a care package? Would that make you feel better?"

"Yes, please! I'd love that." I feel like I can smile a little. "How is it over there?"

"It's different … in a good way. And it's made me see how we can be from two places at once. Kind of weird, huh?"

Lainey tells me she's met some of our extended family and saw one of the lolos we knew growing up, an old family friend here who moved back.

"Solar eclipse in a couple weeks! Are you and Tatang ready for the sun to go down?"

I'd completely forgotten. He'll be leaving us not long after that.

"Lainey, do you think Tatang will miss..." I want to say the word *us*, but that's dumb—I know he'll miss us. "Do you think he'll miss California?"

"Of course he will." She shrugs. "But now that I've seen where he's from, I get it. We've had him to ourselves for a long time, Kaia. This country is a part of him, and there's a world of family and other people waiting for him here."

Even though we're separated by screens, we can still look each other in the eyes—and I know she's telling me the truth.

We talk more about his move, though mainly it's me talking as she listens and nods and asks questions. It's almost like we're in the same room together instead of across oceans. My heart swells, and for a little while I forget about losing.

25

It's Saturday morning and probably everyone in the world is sleeping in but me. How can I when Tatang's all packed? Goodbye parties and goodbyes are the final things on the chalkboard list.

I creep downstairs, where Tatang's at his normal kitchen spot, wearing his pj's, reading the paper, and eating his daily warm pandesal with black coffee.

"Good morning," I say.

He holds the newspaper up and points to a section. "Look . . . the Beach Season film festival is open to the public. They're screening the winning youth movies this morning at the pier."

"Nice. For them," I say.

Tatang wags his finger at me. "I hear that sarcasm, young lady. Anak, those kids worked hard like you and your classmates did. Let's go to the premiere to support them. I'll get us tickets. It says the attire is 'dress in your summer best' and I've got just the outfit."

I'd rather do anything else, but I smile. We don't talk as I eat breakfast, then help Tatang tidy up the kitchen.

The doorbell rings and I excuse myself to answer. I open the door to Trey wearing shorts and a T-shirt printed to look like a tuxedo, and Abby in a pretty flowery sundress.

I roll my eyes.

"Tatang!" I shout. "Your guests are here!"

"Just in time," Tatang says, and when I look he's already changed into his shirt with the red-and-white popcorn buckets all over.

"I can't believe we're going to do this," Trey whispers. "You're lucky Big T is so persuasive."

Abby says, "If you ask me, Tatang's right. I think we should see what the committee thinks a winning film is so we can get some inspo for next time."

"Next time?" I say. Tatang will be on the other side of the globe by then.

"That's the right attitude, Abigail. Success means learning how to improve."

"Go get ready," Abby says.

I look from her face to Tatang's and groan. "All right. Fine."

"Make sure to tell your parents where we're going," Tatang adds.

I come back downstairs wearing my favorite *Eat, Sleep, Art, Repeat* T-shirt with a comfy skirt and Lainey's old sandals. This is as frilly as I get for something we didn't win.

Tatang pops on his fedora, extends his arms to Abby and Trey, and off we go.

• • •

Our first official movie premiere has a real red carpet with a hint of shimmer and everyone dressed in their summer best—except it's not for us. Still, we're here. We showed up.

The event takes place at an old warehouse on the pier. A big banner reads *Welcome to the Beach Season Youth Category Premiere!*

They stamp our hands with a palm tree at the door. As soon as we step inside I see how fancy this thing is. Waiters in tuxedos walk around with trays of tiny food on toothpicks, and a photographer wearing a badge snaps one of us. There's a projection screen that takes up a whole wall, and rows and rows of chairs.

"What do their movies have that ours doesn't?" Trey nods his head toward a bunch of dressed-up kids near the stage who can't stop grinning.

"That girl in the orange skirt lives in my building. She's in ninth grade," Abby says.

I watch those kids get all the attention and it makes me a little jealous. It's how I pictured what winning would look like, only with us up there.

Someone announces that people should take their seats. We choose a back row.

The program starts with intros and how the arts are so important to youth and blah blah blah. The winning teams line the stage and the audience cheers wildly as their individual names get announced.

Tatang takes my hand.

He would have loved seeing me up there. He would have raised his phone to take pictures and would have started a standing ovation for us. Now the only thing he'll remember is how he had to drag me here to teach me one of his lessons about good sportsmanship.

"I'm going to the restroom," I whisper, and I get up to leave.

• • •

I lean against the pier's railing and stare down at the ocean and beach below. The waves crash in and out, strong and bold. Today they look tall and unstable, the kind that Dad would probably want to surf but Mom would get scared of.

I wish we hadn't come here this morning—it's only reminding me that Tatang's leaving soon. Somehow I messed up . . . big time. I text a few sad faces to Lainey, even though she probably won't see them.

Lainey and Tatang are super close, although I can remember once when Lainey felt embarrassed that he lived with us. I was six or seven and she was in middle school. On her birthday she wanted to invite her friends for a sleepover and asked my parents if Tatang could spend the night at Uncle Roy's during the party.

"He's so embarrassing. He's always trying to tell us stories like we're little babies," she said to Mom. "Why does he have to live with us? Why can't we be a normal family like all the other kids?"

I don't know if Tatang ever heard their argument, but I remember Mom got so angry. Lainey told me that no one she knew had old people living with them and she didn't want to be the weird one. My sister feels awful about that memory now.

But I remember thinking the opposite. I was the only kid at school with someone at home who knew every good monster story, which I'd repeat to everyone at recess. They'd say they wish they had a tatang, too. Trey and Abby always wanted to come over because of him and he loved that—so did I.

An arm drapes over my shoulder. "Hello, anak. Beautiful out, huh? Days like this are my favorite." Tatang looks all around at the sky, the sun... at me. He inhales deeply the way he does whenever we're outside. "Shall we go back now so we don't miss the rest of the movies?"

I look him directly in the eyes.

"I'm sorry, Tatang."

"For what?"

"That we didn't get into the festival."

"You're still thinking about that?"

How can I not?

"Winning was supposed to make you so proud of me."

"Oh, my dear Kaia, I don't care about that. I care that you put your whole heart into this. That's what I love the most."

"I guess I also thought . . . I thought somehow if we won you'd change your mind about leaving. You helped me so much on the movie that I hoped you'd see that I need you here." These thoughts seem silly now.

"What did I tell you before? This isn't goodbye."

"No, but you're still leaving."

"Shall I tell you a story?" he asks.

"I don't feel like one right now."

"Can we play the noticing game?"

I shake my head—I'm not in the mood. But he closes his eyes.

For a long moment I stare at him, the smile around his eyes still coming through even though they're shut. I close mine too.

The things I notice: muted carnival music coming from the rides, my hair blowing across my forehead, the crash of waves. Everything like normal. No matter what I'm doing or feeling, life keeps going.

"I'm picturing my happiest memory," Tatang says. "Can you picture yours?"

Hearing the ocean reminds me of a road trip we took to Big Sur when Tatang helped Lainey and me collect armfuls of shells. I was about seven or eight. We walked the water's edge and stopped where the elephant seals gather, piled high, napping in the sunshine. The three of us tried to get near but they started honking at us. We dropped our treasures and took off running and scream-laughing down the shore.

Each perfect day of my life has had the same things: sunshine, waves, and my family near. How will I ever have that again without Lainey and Tatang? Everything's changing.

"Open your eyes," Tatang says. When I do, he's looking at me. "You were able to see something in your past but standing right here, someplace else. We can be aware of the past, the future, and the present, all at once. Do you know what that means?"

I want to know this feeling. I want to hold on to it. If Tatang can go for the more challenging choice after all he's been through, then I need to try.

"What?" I say.

"It means that I am always with you."

Trey and Abby stand by my sides. I'm not sure how much of that they saw, but they saw some of it, because they look at me like I'm a stray puppy they want to take care of.

"Did we miss all the movies?" Tatang asks.

Trey rolls his eyes. "You didn't miss a thing."

"Yeah. This festival proved that we all have different tastes in art," Abby says. "Anyway, we'll get in next year."

We walk down the boardwalk in a chain, arms linked, and along the way stop at a soft serve stand. We find an empty space on the sand. I draw a heart and we root ourselves, licking our ice cream and watching Pier Pressure looping around the same way summer comes and goes.

I focus on the horizon.

"Tatang, tell me a story," I used to say. I would wait for his laugh to start, then to spread.

I'd ask so. Many. Questions.

"Can a person swallow sunshine?"

If they open their mouth wide enough.

"Why is water wet?"

It just is.

"Why don't frogs eat onions?"

Because cake tastes better.

What was your happiest day ever ever ever?

Any day like this. Any day with you.

• • •

When we get home I feel drained. As I go up the front walk behind Tatang, a package sits at our doorstep. Tatang picks it up and hands it to me—it's got my name on it. Must be Lainey's care package. That was fast.

I grab and hug the box. Even from far away my sister's cheering me up.

Tomorrow we throw Tatang his big farewell. Then, his birthplace calls him home.

I lost. He leaves. Summer ends.

26

Tatang's going-away only turns official once we've thrown a big Filipino party. Mom runs between the kitchen and dining room, setting out large trays of appetizers. The party makes me forget about how sad I am, with all the decorations, delicious food smells, and Tatang's favorite tunes playing. I give the house its finishing touch—a banner on the fireplace mantle:

See You Soon!

The doorbell rings. It's our neighbors. Right behind them are our pals from Ocean Gardens—Harold, Cynthia, and several others. "Joy! Kaia!" says Harold, hugging me and Mom. A steady stream, everyone bringing something—a dish, a pink dessert box, flowers—shouting as soon as they spot him, "Don't leave, Celestino!" Trey, Abby, and their families come too, and so do my guests—Mom's students. I suggested we invite them and she said, "What a wonderful idea, Kaia!"

Some of the lolas flutter about, asking who wants what to eat and bringing people to the dining table. Guests load their plates with Filipino and American dishes and settle into the backyard. Mom rented tables with umbrellas and they fill up fast. Tatang travels to each one, making everybody feel welcome and soaking up the attention.

Avery comes over.

"You ready, Kaia?"

My hands shake a little. "Not really. I'm bad at making speeches."

"Speak from your heart."

Outside, people finish their plates and Uncle Roy sets up a microphone with a stereo and little television on the patio.

I go up to him. "Are you starting karaoke now?"

"You joining me in a duet?"

"No, but I... I have something... an announcement I put together for Tatang."

He beams. "Well, look at you. Go ahead, it's all set up now. You need an assist?"

Uncle helps me place a chair in the middle of the patio and I pluck Tatang from the crowd and ask him to sit.

"What's all this?" Tatang asks.

"You'll see."

It's now or never.

I take the microphone and stare out at a yard full of people I love. Nobody notices me, so I tap the microphone. It screeches with feedback.

"May I have everyone's attention, please?" I say, but the yard's full of talking. "Excuse me," I say louder. Faces peer my way.

Dad gives me a *What's going on?* look.

"I've planned a little presentation for Tatang, so if you'll all take your seats, please. Toby and crew, come on up."

A few of the younger cousins take Toby's hand and walk to the patio. Toby hangs a fresh lei that one of our aunties made over Tatang's head.

The younger cousins line up and I hand them the mic.

When I was little the aunties and uncles always made us kids perform at gatherings—the only thing I ever hated about our parties. Today's an exception.

"One, two, three, go!" I say. The cousins shout:

> *You better be believing*
> *That Tatang soon is leaving!*
> *We don't want you to go!*
> *So here, eat some halo-halo!*

Everyone cracks up, and they bow. Toby runs back into the crowd, straight into our dad's arms.

I take the mic again, and people I've known my whole life stare at me. My stomach churns but I remind myself: this is for Tatang.

I spot Mom's students and wave them up. They form a half moon around Tatang, and I introduce them.

First, Avery shares the story of how Tatang spoke to their class and how it inspired them.

"I went home and asked my grandparents to tell me about

the day they came to America and I recorded their stories," Avery says.

"I interviewed my parents about growing up in the Philippines. We never talked about it before and I'm happy we finally did," says the falling-asleep headphones guy, and he hands the microphone back to me.

"I've been thinking a lot about my Tatang leaving," I say, hearing the shakiness in my own voice. "He's the only great-grandpa I've ever known. I don't want you to leave, Tatang. I can't imagine our house without you in it every day, but the thing is…"

I look out at the audience and Mom's tearing up.

"The thing is, you've given our family so much, like a loving home and our start in this country, and the only reason I'm here is because of you. You taught me how to dream. I'll miss you, but I'm glad you're getting to go home. You're my home, and that's what makes it okay, because that will never change. And I hope we can visit you during breaks instead of going to Disneyland." Everyone laughs.

"Thank you, anak," Tatang says.

I take a flat dark velvety box from my pocket. It's larger than my palm. The package at our door yesterday wasn't from Lainey—it was this.

"I spent the summer trying to find the perfect going-away gift for you, and that didn't work out, but I have something else. Mom's student Avery helped me." I open the case to show him. "It's a Congressional gold medal for the time you served in the war. You went through a lot and, well, it doesn't make up for the years you weren't recognized and all you went through, but it's to thank you ... for all the sacrifices you've made. I'm proud of you, Tatang."

I hand him the box.

Carefully, Tatang lifts the medal. It catches the light and glints.

"Read it," I say.

On one side the medal has three Filipino American soldiers wearing battle gear. It reads:

FILIPINO VETERANS OF WORLD WAR II

He flips it to the other side:

UNITED STATES ARMY FORCES IN THE FAR EAST
DUTY TO COUNTRY
BATAAN & CORREGIDOR
LUZON
LEYTE
SOUTHERN PHILIPPINES
1941 1945 1946
ACT OF CONGRESS 2016

For the first time in my life, it seems that my great-grandpa has no words. He holds the medal up to his heart and presses it there as everyone starts cheering and clapping. Dad has

Toby on his shoulders and Mom's next to them, crying. Uncle Roy hugs her.

One by one the college students walk up to Tatang, taking his hand, bringing it to their foreheads, and saying, "Mano po." It means "Your hand, please." It's a traditional Filipino way to receive the blessing of an elder. Tatang looks at me and his eyes fill with tears.

"My dear Kaia, you make me burst with happiness. You always have and you always will."

Abby's filming, and I'm glad. Except for Mom's students, I hadn't told anyone about the surprise, and I forgot to ask someone to record this. I'm sure my family will watch it many times, but I don't think I'll ever need to watch it again to hold this feeling.

27

Tatang, my parents, Toby, and I pack into the minivan and drive to the Children's Science Museum downtown.

I grab a program that says *Eclipse Party!* as we walk into the museum's grassy outdoor area. All kinds of people mill about to celebrate the rare occasion when the sun disappears. There's good stuff in tents, like making your own pinhole camera and "Ask an Astrophysicist." We peek into that one and see scientists in lab coats standing around chatting.

"Ooh!" Dad says as he marches up to one of them.

We spot a huge basket of viewing glasses. "Let's claim ours," Tatang says. He hands me and Mom a pair of flimsy paper shades and helps Toby with his.

"Thanks," I say. I push mine on and we step outside the tent.

"Look up, what do you see?" Tatang asks.

We all look up.

"Hmm ... nothing yet," Mom says as Dad joins us. He has his glasses on too.

That's when I spot it.

"There! It's happening!" The sun's in the sky, big and round and bright, but it's as if a black circle is starting to slide over it. And even though it's darkening, the light's still there, peeking through. It will never go out entirely.

All around us people tilt their heads to the sky in awe.

• • •

After the eclipse party we drive to Camp Art Attack for our movie premiere. We walk up to the high school auditorium when I spot it: a real red carpet!

"May I?" Tatang asks, and he offers me his arm.

The auditorium buzzes. It's not the same as winning a big contest, but it's pretty awesome. Trey and Abby and I are going back to Ocean Gardens before school starts to screen our movie, and Tatang will join by video conference—Cynthia and Harold's idea.

There's a giant projection screen and lots of balloons and chairs set up. Lainey would love it, so I take a quick picture to send.

"You guys made it!" I hear a familiar voice.

What? I scan the crowd—

"Lainey!" I gasp.

She flings her arms around me. I have no idea why she's back early, but my parents must have known because they hook their arms around each other's waists and smile as they watch us, letting me get the first hug.

"I can't believe you're here!" I say.

Out of nowhere I feel the weight of this summer, with all its ups and downs coming at me from every direction. My eyes get tingly. I do the only thing I can: bury my face into my sister's shoulder and feel every moment of sadness and joy.

Lainey steps back, holding my hands. "I'm happy to see you. Sorry I missed the eclipse, Kai-Kai. Uncle Roy was picking me up at the airport."

"We went out for root beer floats instead," Uncle Roy says, squeezing my shoulder.

"Saved you some cool glasses." I hold them up and she laughs. "Why are you back early?" I ask.

"I had to be at your premiere! And I couldn't let Tatang leave without the three of us hanging out first…. Share Bears tonight… big-time!"

"This was all your sister's idea," Dad says to me.

"Yep. I was starting to get so homesick!" she says. "But the main reason I'm back is because I wanted to have more sister adventures before college starts." We beam at each other. "You'll have to surf in the Philippines without me, Tatang. At least until we can all get over to see you."

It would have been just the two of them at the end of Lainey's trip, and she gave that up—for me.

"I'll be waiting," Tatang says, putting his arms around us both.

"Everybody, please take your seats," Eliza says. Abby and Dave sit next to each other and I think I see their elbows touching.

The movies begin, and after each one we hoot and give a standing ovation. When we get to ours, my family laughs so hard at the bloopers. It's Tatang who jumps up from his seat and starts the applause as our credits roll.

After celebrating all the movies we head home, where Mom and Uncle Roy cook a Filipino meal (ube cupcakes for dessert, naturally) and Lainey and I make sure Tatang's packed properly for his trip in a few days. We follow our dinner with swim time in the pool, thanks to Dad, who pushes me and Lainey in.

"Family, you wear me out . . . in the best way," Uncle Roy says. "I should go. I need my beauty sleep." He draws me and Lainey into a huge hug before leaving.

Mom lets us stay up super late. We build a blanket fort in Lainey's room, big enough for us, Tatang, and Toby, and bring in flashlights and a giant bowl of popcorn.

"Who's ready for a story?" Tatang shouts.

"Hold on—don't start without me!" I sprint to my room, grab my phone and a small tripod, and squeeze back under the tent to set it all up. I hit record. "Okay . . . go!"

Tatang looks into the lens. "Have I told you the one about the mango tree from my childhood home?"

"You would climb it and read comics from the highest branch," Lainey says.

"But only after I offered food and prayers to the engkantos who lived there. I didn't want any bad luck to come my way."

He flicks on a flashlight under his chin and makes the creepiest face. Lainey, Toby, and I howl.

If there's anything my great-grandpa taught me, it's to ask questions—loads of them—and we do that for hours:

What would happen if you didn't bring the engkantos food?

What was it like riding a plane to California your first time?

What's the thing you can't wait to see when you return home?

Home. I get it now. Home is this very feeling.

Tatang tells us every story he knows. Toby falls asleep across my lap and I stroke his hair. Even Mom and Dad squeeze in and we all hoot until the fort fluffs down around us, the sounds of my family filling every part of me.

28

The airport is packed with people going in every direction, each one with a story to tell. We're not allowed past the security checkpoint, so we say our farewells near the escalator. Tatang wants to make them quick.

"How do I look?" he asks.

"Ready for first class," Uncle Roy says. Mom and Dad upgraded his ticket so he'd have a comfortable ride home.

After all the hugging and crying and Mom telling him to text us the second he lands, Tatang says: "I'll see you at Christmas, Kaia."

"What?" I look to my parents.

"Booked our tickets the other night," Dad says with a smile.

I start jumping up and down. Lainey gives Tatang a high-five and I give him one more huge embrace—that's the good part of goodbye.

With that, my great-grandfather shuffles into the crowd, his shirt of flowers in every color and purple sneakers making him stand out. Halfway up the escalator he turns and waves. He mouths *I love you.*

• • •

After the airport we snake up the highway, a sparkly ocean blurring to one side. The car's loaded up: towels, surfboards, sunscreen.

Dad rolls down the windows.

"Okay, everyone, take a deep breath!"

Lainey snorts in as loudly as she can and we all bust up.

On the beach I trace a heart and plant myself inside it, watching my family run into the water, waves chasing them over and over again. Uncle Roy swings Toby in circles and my parents hold hands, foam lapping at their ankles. Lainey paddles out solo on her board until I can only see her shadow framed by light.

A plane flies overhead and I wonder what Tatang's doing right now. Probably making friends with the passengers in his row. All kinds of thoughts hit me: how different home will feel, that I start seventh grade soon, how maybe Trey and Abby and I can enter another contest sometime.... Then I remember:

Kaia, where are your feet?

I dig them into the rich, warm sand.

I'm here, my family near and far and always a part of me no matter where I am.

I stare out at the waves, rolling in a regular rhythm like a heartbeat. Even though I'm one small person beside the ocean, it makes me feel a part of something big.

I imagine a movie camera looking down on me, then zooming out-out-out as wide and far as it can go until it reaches a million miles away, and I dissolve into a small blue marble. The Earth.

I close my eyes. The sun wraps me in its warmth. I'm ready for anything and everything.

ACKNOWLEDGMENTS

A favorite childhood tradition of mine was when my family would sit around during gatherings to share Filipino folklore and history. My cousins and I got to hear all kinds of tales, everything from how my grandparents would leave food out for the engkantos (nature spirits) that lived in their tree (for good luck, of course), to our Papang's brave memories of surviving the WWII Bataan Death March, to my family's first moments in the United States. It wasn't until later in life that I realized how meaningful it was to have these deep-seated stories—and to carry them with me. They're every bit a part of who I am and how I see the world. *Any Day with You* came about because I wanted to ask the question: How do our family histories take root? What a joy to explore this through Kaia's (very creative!) eyes.

I have many people to thank for the making of this book!

Much gratitude to my editor, Wendy Lamb, and to associate

editor Dana Carey for their genius, patience, trust, care, and support. Wendy, thank you for helping me get to the heart of this story. This book changed drastically from the first draft to the last, and I'm grateful to have learned so much from you through every iteration.

My appreciation to the always brilliant and lovely Sarah Davies, agent extraordinaire, for continuing to guide me through this journey.

My admiration to designer Michelle Cunningham and illustrator Rebecca Mock for this book's gorgeous cover, and a massive thanks to everyone at Random House, especially dynamic publicist Sydney Tillman and the Random House Children's Books School and Library team.

Writing can feel a little too solitary at times, and I'm thankful for the writer and librarian friends who've been so generous with their encouragement, and in lending their keen eyes to early portions of this novel: Cindy Baldwin, Cathy De Leon, Florante Ibanez, Amanda Rawson-Hill, Rachel Rodriguez, and Rachel Sarah.

I've met many passionate educators along my publishing journey. Thanks for all that you do—and for championing my stories to your students!

Thank you to my supportive parents, Restie and Tina, who on countless occasions have given me the gift of writing and revision time while hanging out with my boys and being awesome grandparents.

Finally, all my love and appreciation to Mark, the most patient and caring life partner I could ever ask for. And to our boys Alden and Cael, thank you for helping me see the world through your love, your imagination, and your big ideas. You three are my home, always.

ABOUT THE AUTHOR

Mae Respicio's debut novel is *The House That Lou Built,* which received the Asian/Pacific American Librarians Association Honor Award in Children's Literature and was an NPR Best Book of the Year. Mae lives in the San Francisco Bay Area with her husband and two sons. Like the main character in this book, she grew up hearing Filipino folktales and history from her family—though it wasn't until much later that she learned to start asking questions.

maerespicio.com